Chapter One.

The sun hid under a patch of grey clouds casting dull rays on the silent street below. The trees that always swayed stood still in the whispering wind. The street was in such a state of silence that even the jangling of keys made little noise. Every human present on Praxton Avenue stood with hands to their mouths at the early present morning.

It was supposed to be a normal fall morning, when shops opened, restaurants collected fresh produce from arriving trucks, and tour guides led groups of people dressed for the desert area to get a head start on seeing the sights of the ever-elusive city of Las Vegas. Yet it was supposed to be a wretched day by all standards. The temperature should have been cooling off to sweater worthy temperatures, but a heat wave had the blistering summer sticking around longer than usual. But the summer was the last thing Las Vegas needed to be concerned with. A new level of horror, even by Las Vegas standards, had been discovered early this morning.

"Let's move," sighed the man at the wheel. He peered through the windshield at the scene in front of him. All Nick Stone saw was a horror show and a whole lot of work. He caught his reflection in the side mirror and ran his hands through his salt and pepper hair.

"What do you think happened here?" Allen Bolton, his partner, catcalled in disbelief.

"Don't know…" He pursed his lips, tugging his maroon tie. "I guess we're about to find out." There was something to be said about Nick Stone. He was a man with a name that fit. He had black hair greying at the sides, cheeks full of stubble, and blue eyes that were grey in the morning light.

He popped the door of the black Ford SUV open like a bubble bursting. The street came alive in mumbles and commands, sirens and shuffling of feet.

"Another fucked up Las Vegas day," he said, swallowing the last gulp of hot coffee. With a shake of his head, he moved with a sluggish gait toward the gathered crowd, choosing to brave the officials first. He saw Sergeant Rick Muller before the lean-faced, sullen-eyed man could see him. He paced behind the crowd in his champagne suit, eyes straight and hands in his pocket.

If Nick felt that his outfit was too classy for a day out in the streets, he said nothing and gave him a curt nod when their eyes met. "Sergeant." He took his hand in a firm shake.

"Detective," Rick greeted back with a nod of his own.

"Always a pleasure to hear from you," smiled Nick, returning his hand to the pocket of his leather jacket, then he tugged at his tie. "Jumped right out of bed this morning at the sound of your voice."

"Don't be so nice, Stone." came the exasperated sigh of Sergeant Rick.

"I'm always nice before 9:00 AM." He smiled at the lie, knowing Sergeant Rick saw through his facade.

"I ordered for the two of you," Sergeant Rick muttered, glancing behind Nick at Allen who was stepping off the SUV. Nick turned to see his partner wave a greeting at Sergeant Rick. "Shall we wait for him?"

"Yes." Nick returned his gaze to Sergeant Rick with a smirk, mischief playing in his grey eyes. "Between the two of us, he has the stronger stomach for blood before 9:00 AM."

Allen Bolton stepped out of the car, pulling his black Nikon camera out of the back seat. He pulled it around his neck, letting it settle on his chest, and sighed. He too was tired. Not because of the mayhem the police were trying to control but because of the noise. He was never a fan of crowds and their inspecting eyes. They needed to go if Sergeant Rick wanted him to work.

He caught a reflection of himself when he nodded in the direction of his partner. He didn't like the way his shoulders hung and stood up straighter. Sergeant Rick had a hard line on his face that told Allen that someone else was tired.

"Morning, Sarg." He plastered a smile, a weary one, that made the sergeant smile just a bit. "How goes it?"

"It was a fine morning," muttered the Sergeant, releasing his arm from their lock behind his back. "Until I got this call. I've seen a lot during my time in the streets of Las Vegas, but this… this is another level."

"Same," Nick muttered, shifting his weight from one foot to the other. "Now, can we get on with it? Time is of the essence."

"Of course," came the tired reply, which was unusual for the sergeant, Allen noted. "Shall we?"

He pursed his lips and stared at the crowd, a frown gracing his thin lips. His eyes darted from the officers in uniform to the people taking pictures and making videos. It was a cacophony of sounds and it irked him.

"Can you disperse the crowd? Don't need a squabble with the public on our hands." Nick asked the sergeant, placing a hand on his shoulder. A knowing smile passed through them, and he let go of a breath he didn't know he was holding.

"*Always* a pleasure to work with you, Nick," quipped the Sergeant. "You remind me I'm the boss and that I'm old."

"Your words, not mine," laughed Nick. Allen waited for the sarcastic japes the Sergeant was known for. Nick had a way of working his nerves.

"Of course," Sergeant Rick replied solemnly and turned to the crowd. Nick dropped his hand from his shoulder and returned it to the pocket of his jacket.

"What's up with him?" Allen stood at ease, rubbing an itch off his clean-shaven cheek.

"Late-life crisis," mocked Nick with a chuckle. He stopped when he realized that Allen wasn't laughing. "A hard day at work." Nick bounced on his heels, casting a stormy gaze at the crowd that refused to disperse.

When their gaze met again, Allen found that familiar silver fire in Nick's eyes that burned whenever he was turning gears in his head.

"You go ahead, help with crowd control," he urged.

Nick sucked on his bottom lip for a second there and asked, "You okay with that?"

"Of course," he said, emulating the Sergeant.

Nick untucked his hands with a grin. "This would only take a moment." His eyes danced with mischief as he backed away from Allen.

"Be nice," he called after him, but Nick was already in the crowd, his 6'7" frame rising above the people. Some parted for him, some stared, but in the end, they started doing what the officers were ordering them to do. Intimidated by his sheer size and silver stare, he decided to stick around Nick Stone, especially in this line of business.

Time kept passing and Nick was beginning to feel angsty. The sweltering sun was up, making the streets warm up, slowing cooking the fifteen corpses lying in body bags. Each one was once a living person with a laugh and a life, and now a cold and smelly carcass for maggots and vultures.

He pinched the bridge of his nose and stared at the skyline for the fourth time since Allen had started taking pictures and wished he'd brought a can of air freshener and sunglasses as his eyes were killing him in the sun.

He tugged at his tie, loosening it a bit more, and crouched down to speak with Allen who was clicking away on his camera.

"How long must I endure the sun?" He sounded like a little girl.

The clicking stopped and Allen turned with brows arched in disbelief. "As long as it takes for me to take pictures, for you to remember to come out with your glasses, and for us to understand what the hell happened here."

"I hate to burst your bubble, Al, but I did a few rounds with the officers…" He ran a hand around the back of his head and rested it like the brim of a hat on his forehead. "No one heard anything that could have been the cause of this horror show last night. They all claimed it was a normal October morning until the sun revealed the bloodied bodies."

"And you believed them?" The question hung in the air and the clicking returned.

"No," said Nick, "Everyone had a story to tell." The shop owners, the grumpy innkeeper down the road, the chef who begged them to leave the details of the murder outside as he had a queasy stomach, and the people who watched like a pre-Halloween murder mystery aired in their yard.
But the police must leave first and the bodies…"

He caught a glimpse of one with a bashed-in face and felt last night's drink rise in his throat. "The bodies need to be removed, cleaned at the morgue, and identified. That would give us more space and information to work with."

"Maybe so," Allen said and straightened to a stand causing Nick to follow suit. "An autopsy would help too. With this many bodies, I can only imagine what they'd find out,"

"How long it would take," Nick groaned. He had never liked the waiting for intel and the general information pool; he couldn't sit still for it to fill up. "It's taking even longer because of you."

"It's called being thorough," smirked Allen. "You should try it sometimes. Heard it shifts perspectives quite well."

"I'll keep that in mind when...hey!" His eyes were pinned on a young lady leaning on the barricade. She flinched when he called her but didn't back away. Allen lowered his camera and stared at the lady who was bold enough to watch the scene.

She was clad in a short denim skirt, white Converses, and a grey sleeveless shirt, tucked in at the front. Nick noted her hair was black and pulled into a ponytail, but when the wind blew, he caught a glimpse of blonde.

As lovely as her legs were to stare at, she wasn't supposed to be there–her lack of a badge or a uniform showed that much. She addressed him with an aloof smile and continued studying the corpse.

He bit back a curse at her dismissal and cracked a disdainful smile on his face. "This is a homicide scene, Bambi, not a set for The Real Housewives of Las Vegas. Run along now,"

His comment turned her green gaze on him. "I wasn't looking for fake reality TV." *Oh, we have a firecracker in our midst.* He found her boldness admirable. It was obvious that she didn't know how wrong she was right now. He could easily put her in jail, and yet…

"And I wasn't looking to start a conversation with a prissy high schooler," he snapped. "Leave, else I tag you as a suspect or arrest you for contaminating the scene."

"You can't do that," she shrugged. "I'm not even in your scene." She spread out her hands to show she was standing outside the restricted area. "But then again…" She paused, picking up two paper bags by her feet. He hadn't noticed that. "The whole Praxton Avenue should be your crime scene. It took someone long enough to do something big here. I'll bet you five bucks you could find a weapon of some sort around if you know where to look."

Nick glanced at Allen. He had his camera pressed to his face, but he was sure his ears were tuned to what she had babbled. "Or not," she continued. "Anyone who took time to arrange those bodies is thorough enough to not leave any weapon lying around."

There's that word again! He thought and turned to see a smile on Allen's cheek. *Smug, are we?* No matter how smart-mouthed she was, she was a distraction that needed to go. "I didn't ask for it."

He realized that she was gone the same moment Allen took to his feet in a jolt. "Of course!" he cried. "She's right."

Chapter Two.

The room was captured in a certain stillness that moved dust off the ground and into your brain. The fan above spun too fast for its faulty connection, whirling like a controlled hurricane–and yet it was still not enough to beat back the sweltering heat.

When they had returned, Allen did his best to clean up. Little good that did; the relentless sun peeking from the open windows filled the room with light, highlighting they needed to clean, which Nick had done with a grimace more suited for a corpse. He never got to finish it though before he grumbled, "I would have figured it sooner if Miss Cute Ass didn't butt in."

With a red magnetic placeholder hanging in midair over a transparent board, Allen watched the red-faced Nick. "I know you would." He turned to retrieve a picture and placed it with the others on the board. "There is no one in Las Vegas with a better eye."

"Thank you," agreed Nick, a little too smugly as he normally expects smart ass remarks.

"Though a little slow but far more superior than Miss Cute Ass," he quipped, taking a step back to admire his work. Thirty freshly printed pictures stood in two rows of fifteen. The top row focused on the major injury site of each corpse and the bottom was an aerial view of the bodies as they had been found.

He heard the scuffling halt. "It was staring at our faces all along." He looked over his shoulders to find Nick pacing behind him, his broom abandoned.

"Yes, we could say she arrived in the *nick* of time."

"How funny," Nick appeared at his side that moment, with a joyless grin.

Standing side by side, Allen felt rather smallish with his height of 6'2" and a less muscular physique. He did alright on his own but with curly blonde hair tumbled down past his collar and brown eyes hidden in clear glasses, it was easy to mistake him for Nick's slightly less attractive brother.

"She wasn't a protege in any right," continued Nick, still with a scowl on his face. "Anyone could see that all the victims were moved to Praxton Avenue."

"By whom and why there?" muttered Allen. *The murderer of fifteen people? Or an accomplice?* He has pondered this very thought while he treated the photos in the basement.

"Look here," he said and pointed at the lower row. "You were right. All the victims died from injuries that they couldn't have caused themselves; these were all murders."

Nick crossed his bulky arms against his chest with a smirk that Allen caught. "Don't look too cocky. We haven't found any truth as to the type of injury and the possible murder weapon."

"Looking cocky is part of my job." He dropped his hands to his hips. "Cleaning is not."

Allen chuckled, making way for his swivel seat by the window. "Not in the slightest bit." Nick had been attempting to clean up since they had returned from the homicide scene to no avail. The desks were still littered with paperwork. Dirty dishes and mugs still sat, breeding germs in the kitchen sink, and every trash bin needed to be emptied.

"Thank the stars you're a better detective than you are at staying clean," he teased, expecting Nick's remark. It didn't come. Instead, Nick moved closer to the photo, loosening his tie completely.

"Did you take these shots in any particular order?" muttered Nick, reaching for two pictures with each hand. His eyes were set on something Allen couldn't make out.

"No, if you rule out the way I found them," answered Allen, leaning into his seat. "Why the sudden interest?"

"Notice how some of the injuries are similar…"

"No. No, I do not." He was out of his chair in the next second. "Hey, be careful with those; they're still moist," he cautioned while unpinning the photos of the injuries.

Nick gave him a smirk that spelled "I'll try" and brought them all down from the transparent board before he reached the table. Nick was onto something; Allen could feel it, like a thread tugging his gut.

"Notice the similarities," he said and pulled out two pictures, placing them side by side.

Allen stared down at Nick, moving the photos repeatedly until he had three groups of five.

"No," he shook his head, "I don't see anything."

"Must I spell everything out for you?" Nick's mouth fell open. He licked his lips in an agitated scoff and moved away from the table.

Allen chuckled at his dramatics and moved closer to the table. He began placing the pictures back on the board the way Nick had rearranged them. With arms lifted to pin the last picture, he paused, held it for closer inspection, and turned to Nick who was leaning on the wall by the kitchen door with arms crossed and another smug smile.

"You son of a–"

"Save it." Nick pushed himself off the wall, stepping forward to hang the photo himself. "Question is, are we looking at one killer with a creative streak? Or three with a taste for theatrics?"

"Don't know…" Allen hummed, rubbing the back of his neck, "but it's a start."

They stood there in the same spot, mulling over theories, pacing and clenching fists, all to no avail.

"Fuck, this is annoying!" Nick ran a hand through his greying hair and turned to Allen by the swivel chair. "We aren't making any progress."

Allen gave him a weak smile. "A lead is still a lead. We just need to make it wider, bigger…"

"Clearer," muttered Nick. "How about another round of tete a tete."

Allen dropped to the seat with a tired sigh at the thought of going out to speak with more people again. "It's our best start, but maybe we should wait for their records first. Silas said he'll send it in as soon as he gets it."

"Alright then," Nick nodded, tugging on his cuffed sleeves, "I can wait." He matched up the staircase that led to the apartment and disappeared.

Allen let out a breath he was holding and dropped his head to the headrest. He closed his eyes to find solace only to find thoughts of the day dancing between his eyes. How he had arrived at an untidy office and a semi-sober Nick who offered no explanation and how he had been trying to clean up before Sergeant Rick called. How he had moved from door to door, trying to talk to the locals about the case…

Hasty footfalls on wood made him groan. He peered through heavy eyelids to find Nick in an army green tee shirt that highlighted the fact that he wasn't out of the game and a pair of form-fitting dark jeans cuffed at the ankles above suede Vans.

"Where are you off to?" he muttered, shutting his eyes.

"Nowhere I shouldn't be going…" came Nick's reply. "Nowhere I can't go."

He scoffed at Nick's cryptic words. They both knew he was off to complete whatever madness he was up to the previous night. If they didn't have a case, he would have let him go easy but they needed all their wits.

"I thought you were still tidying up?" he sighed, remembering the broom Nick had left by the door. "Whatever happened to 'no partying on a case'?"

Even as he spoke, he knew he was wasting his voice. Nick was his own man, but still… He peeled his eyes open to an empty room, with the noise from the street and the whirling fan that rose dust as his music.

What a day! What a day indeed, he thought, rising from the seat before sleep overtook him.

***

It was Nick's philosophy to never fight the current of your life. To go with the flow.
"Work with it…" he often said, "and it would work for you."

Even when he was knee-deep in deadlines, work, and stress, halfway in need of a drink, ten hours of sleep, or a good fuck, he kept to his philosophy. It had never steered him wrong all forty-seven years of his life. Maybe once… But his hands were clean in Edith's case. Everyone knew that.

So, when he sent out the job offer for a secretary, he was just going with the flow. Yes, Allen was the flow, but he chose to succumb this time, with a little bit of his flair, which involved choosing the first twenty-three-year-old that applied and scheduling an interview.

He sat at a white table across from an empty white seat. It was a strategic place to sit because it gave him a good view of the office. He had tidied up the best he could when he returned from the station early, with another matter on his mind. One look and whoever was coming might have a feel of her new job.

His real reason for sitting there was to get a good glimpse at the girl before she noticed that he was there.

He dropped his boots from the table when he saw someone by the door. The bell rang and the door clicked open. He saw the girl walk in. "Hello," she called out in a quiet, uncertain voice as she walked into the foyer. "It's Lisa. Lisa Monroe. I was invited for an interview… for the office of a secretary."

Black hair… nice frame, he observed. Voice soft enough to sing me to sleep. He caught her maroon body con dress and heard the clacking of heels on the wood. Yes, he'd made another fine choice, as always. If she looked pretty, did her job, and worked well with Allen, he was fine with her.

Making noise with his seat, he got up. "Hello?" called the girl, louder now. "Anybody there?"

In two steps, he was out in the open with a line on his lips about her first lesson with working with private investigators, but his comment died in his mouth when he saw her face.

"You?!" he chuckled, and at the same time, she gasped, taking a step back like he was going to hit her or something. "What a pleasant turn of events." He smiled.

Chapter Three.

Nick loved watching her squirm; it had been the highlight of his day. Her hands shook when she brought his coffee, and her voice tremored with anxiety whenever he called for her. It was wonderful to watch. Now she knew what he felt when scrutinizing her on the street.

He did notice a few more things that kept him glued to her frame from under his lashes and not to Allen who had walked into the office rather exhausted. Her hair, for instance, wasn't completely black. It was blonde at the tips, blending with the black. And she would smile sometimes for no reason. Not at him, of course, but still, it was beautiful. It was natural, not fake, even if she were trying hard to answer the interview questions the way he wanted to hear them.

After his methodical attempts to make her interview harder to her humiliation, she still wanted to work for him and start immediately. He admired her perseverance and gave her a trial; Nick found himself all the better for it. The office was returned to its original clean design. The scent of freshly made coffee and the cinnamon rolls he ordered her to bake floated in the air–all things he wanted Allen to notice.

***

But it was Lisa who needed them much more than they needed her. She loved this line of work. She hadn't been quite honest with her answers to all the interview questions, specifically her private life. Lisa wanted so badly to be an investigative reporter herself but raising children as a single mother didn't allow for the full-time dedication needed in that line of work. That and she really needed the money. She knew she had a great ass and shapely breasts, and she intended to use them to her advantage. That was until she saw him again.

While she hoped that he didn't notice, she knew she was shaking when she delivered coffee to Nick after he had hired her on the spot. But it wasn't about the job - there was something about him. Ever since she saw him and stayed firm with her on the street, she felt something. Most men ogled at her, but Nick stayed firm and strong, and she respected that… no she admired that.

"Fuck don't do this to me," she mumbled to herself. She was turned on. There was nothing sexual said or hinted at, but there didn't need to be. He was dominant and funny, and although she hadn't had any experience with older men older men, she knew what she liked, and Nick was that guy on the covers of the sexy books she read. "Keep it together, I need this job," she kept thinking to herself.

***

"Who ran you over? Silas, perhaps? Or fifteen corpses?" Nick turned his attention to his partner. "A dead end or a deadline?"

"Both." Allen ran a hand across his hair, shaking the long curls loose. He placed his hands on his hips. His eyes moved from Nick, who sat drinking coffee, to the tables and chairs. He saw the empty baskets and ferns in order as a heavenly aroma danced by.

When his eyes fell on Nick again, a smile bloomed on Nick's face. "You hired someone?"

"As instructed," winked Nick. He saw Lisa emerge from the kitchen with a fresh batch of rolls. "You wouldn't believe who the cat dragged in!?"

"Surprise me," Allen yawned, almost hitting Lisa who was behind him. She stepped back on nimble feet. "Oh…" Nick gave him a sideways nod and a smile to urge him on. He didn't want to embarrass himself, so he straightened up and turned.

He scoffed, swallowing a chuckle and pushed his wire-rimmed glasses up his nose instead. "Well... Aren't you a pleasant surprise?"

Nick forced himself to sit still with pursed lips when she introduced herself and served Allen a plate of cinnamon rolls. She was fidgety–as expected– and moved like a brave cat who was suddenly scared. It amused him.

When she was out of sight, he leaned in the Allen, who took the seat by his right. "Imagine my joy when she walked in," he chuckled. "Revenge has never been so beautiful."

"Revenge can wait." sighed Allen. "If she's going to work for us, you'll have enough time for your petty mind games. Oh, and don't forget we are twice her age so keep your dick in your pants and out of her. For now, we have a case that's filled with dead ends."

"Fair enough," nodded Nick, settling into his seat. He had had a rough time with some family members of the victims.

"Went to see Silas. Two of the victims, Alex Finnigan, male, Caucasian, thirty-two, and Phoebe Gerald, female, Caucasian, twenty-six. Two lovers who liked the on-and-off lifestyle and dabbled in bondage and swinging, which was determined by their phone pictures and internet history. Eight hours into their off period, they were found dead. Imagine that…"

"Imagine that" Nick chuckled. "What a Shakespeare thing, so romantic."

"Families were distraught, as usual." Allen nodded and went for a roll. Taking a bite, a slight smile appeared on his lips. "She's good,"

"I have good taste," smirked Nick, "and a quick mind."

"Where is this going? Didn't you hear me say that she is half our age? You hired her as eye candy and got lucky that she can cook and clean," Allen chuckled.

"Where I want it and where I always wanted it," Nick said, with one brow arched in amusement. He made Allen watch him take a sip of his coffee. And another sip.

Allen laughed, "Take your time, take your time. Just in case the people come for us. You know, because the mayor wants to shut down Halloween this year at Praxton if the case isn't solved before then. I will give them your head. Plus, you are her boss. Fucking employees is certainly against the human resources rules if we had any."

"Yes, I am aware of the time frame and unwritten rules. Unwritten rules are just like written rules and innocent women: made to be broken," he drawled in return. "Sergeant Rick made the timeframe abundantly clear to me in his office this morning. Something about children and security and murder being bad for business." He paused for another sip of his coffee. A distinct flavor of cinnamon exploded in his mouth.

Not that he was complaining, but Lisa was going all out with the fall theme. When he told her to show him what she could do, he didn't think it would be a homey experience. *Cinnamon rolls. Cinnamon latte. What next? Cinnamon bread.*

His thoughts made him chuckle into his drink. Allen scoffed and leaned in for another roll. "Any day now, Nick. With your quick mind, I'm sure we can make up for the lost time. We need to break this open."

"Right." He dropped his boots from the low coffee table and rose to his feet. "Two of the murder victims were lovers. Young. Capricious. Foolish. But perhaps every time they broke up, it was necessary."

"Maybe a fight over a character flaw?" Allen mused, resting his back on the chair.

"Maybe." He nodded again, tugging at the black leather strap of his Rolex watch. "How did the talk with their families go?"

"No one was home for the girl," Allen shrugged. "The brother, a chef, wasn't so happy about it."

"Did the girl have… sisters, aunts, or a friend around her age? Girls tend to talk too much about everything." His mind went to another girl. One who was tinkering about the office.

"She's not a girl, Nick," Allen groaned, pushing himself off the couch. "But I see what you mean. I met a cousin, slightly older. She sat with us and didn't say much though."

"Good," commented Nick. "Call her."

"Call her?"

"Yes." Nick shook his head like it was an obvious thing to do. "Visit the house again… whatever. Just talk to her now while she grieves."

"I will, but later."

"I'll give them *your* head. Now, Allen!"

"Alright, alright," Allen raised his hands in agreement. "I'm not going anywhere though. Silas can dig out her phone number." Snatching the entire plate of cinnamon rolls from the table, he rose to his feet. "These are good. Make sure to tell her that."

"You can tell her that yourself," Nick sneered, dropping back his throne.

"Be nice, Nick. She's a lady, remember, not an arch nemesis, and she works for us. Plus, she is needed." Allen made for his office.

"I'm *always* nice to ladies," He said, shrugging off the pointed look Allen was giving him, "but sometimes they don't want nice."

"That… I believe." sighed Allen. With a soft click, the door to his office opened, revealing a coffee brown mahogany desk–a gift from his mother in California. Within the office were shelves overflowing with books and a board filled with multi-colored sticky papers.

The door closed behind him, and the room was bathed in quietness once again. Nick drained his mug and rose to his feet, then sat back down. "Be nicer, Nick, until they admit they don't want nice," he whispered to himself and let the mug sit on the table for a while.

He shut his eyes and massaged his forehead. The thought of hanging onto straws was getting to him, draining him of his mojo. *One solid lead… just one.* He groaned and rested his head on the headrest.

He opened his eyes to Allen pacing the room. He suppressed a groan when he moved to get up. Rubbing his left shoulder, he asked Allen with a frown, "How long was I out?" His voice came out a croak. Almost as disoriented as he felt.

"Longer than I thought," chuckled Allen. Then he went back to his pacing. He had changed his khakis and blazer for cargo shorts and a plain grey shirt. Even his hair was in a ponytail at the back of his head.

This meant two things: he needed to play a more casual part, somewhere. Or they had closed for the day. Nick chose the latter when he saw the pink and orange sky and the brightening of the lights. He shuffled to the edge of his seat and dropped his head on his waiting palms. But not before noticing his mug was gone.

"And Ms. Monroe?" he mumbled.

"Relived her of manual labor," came Allen's reply. His eyes held a storm when he raised them. "She'll be back tomorrow at 8:00," he chuckled. "I made her promise to make more treats, so be nice!"

"I'll be on my best behavior," smirked Nick. He stretched himself like a cat on the cream-colored couch and tousled his sleep hair even more. Setting his sharp eyes on Allen, he asked, "So… what'd you find out?"

Allen paused and said, "I'm touched by your confidence in me."

"I'm confident in *me*," Nick retorted.

"Ever so humble," Allen chuckled, walking to the seat by Nick's right. "I can't fault you. Not with what I got from the cousin, Julia. Lovely woman. A bit too eager but… she loved Phoebe dearly."

"Skip to the good part," Nick interrupted the useless story Allen was about to tell.

"Find your patience," Allen quipped. "You're going to need it for this one."

"Oh, no. Don't tell me it's a telenovela," he groaned, pinching the bridge of his nose with his thumb and forefinger.

"I must admit, I tried to keep a straight face while she talked–" Allen chuckled as if he had just gone to a comedy club and remembered a joke.

"Wait, you've met with her?" A quizzical look appeared on Nick's face.

"Yes," answered Allen like it was obvious. "And Silas called."

Nick shook his head and rubbed his eyes. "Wait, wait, wait… Hold up. How long was I out?"

"Long enough." Allen sighed. "Stick with black coffee." Nick nodded and settled back into his seat, prodding Allen to continue. "Where was I… oh, yes! The breakups were caused by Ms. Phoebe. Welcomed a lot of exes while she was with Alex. The latest being a Mr. Harrison… or Alex…" Allen let out a deep breath. "It was complicated."

"I can see that," laughed Nick.

"Alex found out about the other man, confronted Phoebe, voices were raised, and they broke up."

"Shocker," mumbled Nick.

"Here's where it gets interesting. Searched for Mr. Harrison. Guess what? He went AWOL two days before the incident."

"Interesting, indeed." Nick's thin lips stretched into a smile. *Now we're getting somewhere.* "Any info on his whereabouts? We could get Silas to track his–"

"Do you underestimate me?" Allen arched a brow at Nick.

"Never," Nick laughed.

"Mr. Harrison boarded a plane for San Francisco last Friday."

"Know where to find him?" Nick leaned forward.

"Working on it." Allen smiled, linking his hands behind his head. "Give me a night."

"We've got one lead. A solid one," Nick grinned. "Now we're getting somewhere."

"And you? Any progress?" Allen asked.

"I've been waiting for you to ask."

***

The sun shone without mercy on the street below it, causing the temperature to rise within the SUV. Even with the air conditioning on, Nick could feel the heat–or rather, knew the heat–he was going to face if he stepped out of the car. But he had to. He had come this far. If he went back now, feigning tiredness or plain bad luck, they'd know he wanted to slack off.

It was his second time on Praxton in the last twenty-four hours, and he wasn't looking forward to it. Killing the engine, he loosened his grey tie just a bit and popped the door open. He heard the screaming first and he knew, there was going to be a third time. *Never a dull moment on Praxton. No, not when Halloween is around the corner and the people want my head. Fuck this!* He sighed and reached for his gun, hidden underneath his suit. *Another fine day ruined.*

Chapter Four.

"What drives ill-meaning people here?" mused Allen. "Could it be that they are riding on the wave of the homicide or is Praxton a place where one commits a crime and gets away with it?"

He walked along the shattered glass, unafraid of large particles piercing through his black leather oxfords. With hands behind his back, he paused his dangerous trekking and turned to the store.

What he knew was that in the heat of noon, broad daylight, a jewelry shop had been robbed. There were three people in the shop, the salesperson was shot dead, a female buyer was shot in the thigh, and a teenage boy who was unscathed physically but visibly upset and in shock. He sat on the bare floor, leaning on the wall, making incoherent babbles while Nick whispered calmly to him.

The police had sealed off the shop when they arrived but had yet cleaned up: glass, blood, and fingerprints were everywhere. Allen sighed with a slow side to side nod and walked over to Nick. He stopped at the foot of the stairs where the boy sat and leaned on the wall. He had opted for a professional look, something to make Lisa's first day memorable. A three-piece grey suit tapered to his fitting - gift from his brother in New York. He rested his sleek form on the wall, pulling Nick's attention to himself.

"Nick Stone has become a hero," he praised his partner. "If you hadn't shown up when you did, we might have had no survivors."

The boy raised his frail face to him, and he saw the tears in his glassy blue eyes, the wrinkles on his scared face, and the dilation of his pupils. *He's still shaken,* he told himself. *Not the best place to talk. Or...*

He nodded for Nick's attention and walked away again to stand by the only untouched glass in the shop–the one with the name etched on it, facing the street. Nick was beside him not a moment later.

"You did good here," breathed Allen to his partner.

"No, I didn't." sighed Nick. "If I had made it here sooner, maybe…"

"The rules of a war zone and those of a seemingly crime-free area aren't the same."

"Yet the laws of time, life and death, remain the same." Nick scoffed and drew in a long breath. "Don't coddle me, Al. I failed. No arrest of the robbers here, and no progress with the case."

"Yes, about that." Allen turned his brown eyes hidden behind clear glasses to Nick with an arched brow. "How did it go?"

"Waste of my time," spat Nick. "Nothing interesting to pin down the group Silas listed out as suspects for one Mr. Pietro."

"You sure about that?"

"Of course, I'm sure. I'm fucking sure!" Nick cursed, his nostrils flaring. His eyes turned stormy–the color of the sky in a thunderstorm before closing them in a soft groan.

"Not here, not now." Allen cautioned. "Maybe you should take a break. I can take it from here. Lisa has some lovely scones filled with pumpkin and sesame seeds waiting for you at the office." Nick set his hooded gaze on Allen. Something in his gaze told Allen that the case and all that was happening around it weighed on his partner like a bag of bricks. Nick would never agree to it though, but he was observant enough to catch it.

"You're right," said Nick in between deep breaths. "Maybe I should take a break but it's not because I like scones,"

"Neither is it about making Lisa uncomfortable." Allen nodded.

"Yeah!" A smile bloomed in slow succession on Nick's face. "I just need a quiet afternoon at the office. And seeing that ass move around should allow me to concentrate, just not sure on what."

"Off you go then," urged Allen as he rolled his eyes, giving a sweeping wave to the door. "Rest but remember to check in with Silas on the people you were watching." *I just want you to be okay.*

"Yes, ma'am," chuckled Nick as he walked on nimble legs past Allen. He greeted the officers discussing by the door and left the scene. It felt quieter and colder without him, Allen noticed, but he shook it off and turned to the boy whose eyes were on the door that Nick had just walked through.

***

The red feathered tail of the dart made a thud as it pinned a few inches off the bullseye. Nick ran his hand through his dark hair, drawing out the frustration from his face. His feet were heavy as he went to retrieve his darts. His eyes were downcast– the storm in them had died out. When the door in front of him opened, he looked up to see a red-faced Lisa.

"I'm sorry for barging in," she managed to say, settling her gaze on the floor.

He sighed and moved closer. "I can hardly call leaving the kitchen 'barging in'." He raised a bare arm and she flinched.

A chuckle settled in his throat at her coyness. He wasn't going to touch her… or was he? She was watching him from under her long eyelashes. He knew she was: he could feel it before but now he could see it.

Instead, he picked his darts one by one off the board above her. She remained between him and his board, transfixed and frozen. He looked down at her with exasperated eyes only to find her low-cut dress rather helpful. They revealed the swell of her firm breasts, which moved up and down with her rapid breathing. He was drawn to it, and she knew it and didn't care.

At that very moment, she raised her eyes with boldness. Her lips appeared inches away from his; a hunger arose in his chest, accompanied by the familiar tightening of his loins. *Shit.* He groaned and the door behind him popped open. They broke apart, entangling limbs and bumping heads in the process, but stood apart, side by side in the end.

Allen stepped through the front door, making his way toward the main reception area which doubled as a recreation room. He paused by the coffee table when he saw them. "You look…better," His eyes trailed over Nick's sleeveless shirt and sweatpants.

"Burned off some steam at the gym," Nick shrugged, pursing his lip, for the pressure in his loins was yet to dissipate, and he knew Allen had keen instincts.

"Good for you," Allen smiled and moved to his office. "Although, I did tell you to rest."

"I *rested*… then got tired of feeling like a sissy." He moved back to his previous position behind the couch.

"Fair enough," Allen chuckled. Turning his attention to Lisa, he asked, "Are you alright?"

She blinked rapidly, reverting to normal. "Yes… yes," came her breathy voice. Those were the words that came out, but her thoughts were saying that she needed to change her panties.

Allen nodded and turned the knob to his office. "Any finding?" Nick asked before he could step in.

"Dead end," he sighed, retrieving a rubber band from his pocket. He tied his curls up in a ponytail and shut his door. "Somehow, something doesn't add up." He moved to the board where he had pinned the photos.

Nick moved closer. "Maybe we're looking at it all wrong."

"How so?" Allen thought with a sigh.

"We know the murders didn't happen exactly where we found the bodies." Nick cocked his head to the right. "And the injuries were in groups of five…" He moved closer to the pinned photos and placed a hand under his chin.

"Look," he said after a moment of silence. "Can I view a zoomed photo… of that one?" He pointed to the middle one of the third row. Allen chuckled at his enthusiasm and pulled his laptop from the satchel around his shoulders.

Nick snatched it while it was still booting and searched for the photos himself. His eyes turned bright like a clear sky, and he laughed. "You've got to see this, Al. Bit by bit, the pieces are making a trail."

"Why am I not surprised?" Allen laughed and retrieved his laptop. Nick had zoomed in on a picture. Allen saw several wounds before Nick could say it. He flipped to the next picture and the next one, the next one, and the next one…

"Why didn't we see this before?" he laughed, dropping the laptop on the coffee table.

"Might have to check the morgue to confirm." Nick smiled wide, lifting his hand to place behind his head. It not only made him taller, but veins popped out on his biceps, making them more noticeable.

"After I return." Allen cocked his head, amusement at the turn of events still in his eyes.

"You know I can't stand gory stuff before 9:00 AM," smirked Nick. "I'll keep myself preoccupied with… more intriguing *stuff* until you return."

Nick had meant to keep his word and focus on the case. Even after Allen had left for an evening with his nieces and nephews, he mulled over the photos and files again - anything to get more information about the murder.

It was a fruitless task. He clenched his fist and took deep breaths. When the storm calmed, he moved for a drink. But storms don't calm so easily, do they? In that instant, Lisa walked in again asking if he needed anything. She was intending to step out to get coffee and fresh air.

"I'd love to, but I think I've had so much in the space of twenty-four hours. I might break down if I don't have real food soon," Nick said, rubbing his hand through his hair.

The tension grew thicker. He wanted food, yes, but he wanted Lisa. She looked too young for her age, which was already half his own. And, of course, she was sexy as hell. He had a thing for petite women, but this was more than just physical attraction. Something about how she reacted to him hit him in places casual fucking cannot.

She acted young and vibrant, but not like in her twenties. More like a young virgin heading off to college who hasn't experienced the world. Innocent, but bold. He liked talking to her but more than that, he liked how she constantly flipped her hair while around him as if constantly trying to pretty herself for a selfie.

"Well, we could order actual food. I'm hungry too. What would you like?" Lisa asked, locking the door behind her and biting her lip. "I'm up for anything," she said, her face turning red. She said it innocently as if she meant food, but her lip biting expanded the meaning.

"Well… I'm not sure. Food, for starters. What do you have?" Nick said, pulling out his credit card from his wallet and piercing her eyes with his stare. "But if you come any closer, I'm afraid I might kiss you, and that might not be a good idea."

"Kiss me, then," were the words she wanted to say, but she just froze and instead put her hands to her sides. Her posture and facial expression changed, as if she went from being his secretary to be whatever he wanted her to be in that moment.

"We're coworkers, I'm your boss, and I'm twice your age. I want to at least be able to look you in the eye without any awkward feeling tomorrow." Those were the words he said but certainly not the words he meant.

"We're adults, aren't we?" She was flipping her hair again, and her face was clearly flushed.

"You don't know what you're getting into," said Nick, "I'm not sure you're ready for someone like me. Plus, like I said, I'm your boss."

"Yes sir, you are" Lisa responded and visibly panted.

Nick didn't move. He smiled but didn't respond other than to keep staring at her. He was holding back. But the words "Yes, sir" coming from her lips began to form an erection in his pants which became clear to Lisa. He knew what he was and what type of woman to fuck. In an instant, all those women his age he had fucked and dominated came to mind as the only thing that made him cum was being a "Dom" to a younger version was his fantasy. Someone who looked and, more importantly, acted like Lisa.

Lisa had never felt like this. Almost as if she had taken some sort of drug, Lisa was high and couldn't think clearly. Nick's presence - and dominance - made her feel something she had never felt before, and she needed to please him. Lisa slowly made her way to him as if under a trance, not able to resist straddling him. Lisa leaned in for a kiss, barely touching his lips. She pulled her head back to see the pleasure on his face. She leaned in and kissed him again. More intense this time, urging him to open up for her.

He was responding, but not fully. He could tell he had her and could do anything he wanted, but he knew it wasn't right. The instant Lisa tried to grab his crotch, he slapped her hand away. "Yes, sir" coming from her lips started it, but this was the point where he lost his mind. He spread his legs and positioned her between them, using his other hand to snag her hair at the back of her neck, pulling her head back while covering his lips with hers. She had initiated the kiss, but Nick took over control with that one move, and she immediately gave in to any movement he was making her do.

She tasted like everything he had imagined, including when he masturbated. Nick was quite obsessive about women. However, there was something about him that made women take note, which was why he never made the first move. His presence and confidence turned women on, and he knew it. By not making the first move, it almost dared women into doing it for him. And it always worked.

He'd give hints and signs that spelled attraction, but he never fully declared how much of a woman he wanted. He'd lure one in, then strike the first chord.

And once she did, he took the lead. Little wonder he was so good at his job.

Sharp, hard kisses parted her lips. His tongue licked over them while thrusting inside her mouth to claim possession in a way he believed no man had ever attempted. The pleasure ripped through his senses like a cascading explosion as she moaned softly, yet loudly, against his mouth. In his mind, his fantasy was playing out directly before him as he had corrupted her. He knew by her strong personality that she would never submit to someone her own age, but in this moment, he didn't care. She was about to be his.

She pulled her hands away from his neck, unbuttoning his white shirt and running his hands through his hard chest. She went further to undo his belts to gain more access. Just then, Nick held her hands, stopping her from going any further.

"You naughty little girl," Nick glared.

"Okay?" she asked almost hopelessly, breathing harshly. Somehow through all the kissing and groping, him calling her a "naughty little girl" almost made her orgasm without even touching. And despite her need for this, his instructions were almost like orders she couldn't resist.

"Mmm-mmm. Not today. Not here."

"Yes... sir," she responded while in her mind she was begging to be fucked.

"Lisa, I must tell you that you don't know what you're getting into. Hell, you're not even ready for this - for me. I think you need to leave for the day," he demanded as he pulled her away, fixed her shuffled hair, kissed her lightly on the forehead, then walked away.

Lisa was aghast, clearly not in her right mind. If this was a boyfriend her age, she would have been upset and angry at her sexual frustration. But somehow with Nick, doing what he told her felt better than just having sex. As if somehow pleasing him meant more than an orgasm.

Nick seemed all too relaxed for the situation, hiding his own sexual frustration. "Little girls shouldn't play grownup games, Lisa. If you must, don't do it with me. There might be no turning back."

But no turning back is exactly what she wanted.

Chapter Five.

As the next day arrived, Lisa dressed a little differently, spending time to pick out an outfit that would ride the line between professional and slutty. She wanted to be desired but not inappropriate. She wanted eyes to be on her more than usual. When she left her house, she was wearing a short blue dress that rode high enough to demand attention but just low enough where she could bend over without her panties showing. The top allowed full view of her cleavage without seeing her bra - black and lacy - which was bought as a set with a black and lacy thong that now rode inside of her ass, making a slight crease as it was very tight. The front was so tight it made a slight crease, too.

She walked into the office, carrying a tray of coffee, each cup holding the person's preference. Nick liked his black and bitter. No cream, no sweeteners. Matched his personality. *How could someone live without taste?* Lisa always wondered. But after what had gone on the other day, Lisa had concluded that Nick was a man that sweet things repelled, including herself.

In the history of her sexual life, there was never a time she had been rejected, or even turned down by anyone. Men followed her like flies. She had this narrative of blocking every means of contact after each encounter, especially if she had made the first move. She knew they'd come back for more, but Lisa doesn't believe in stale things. *Once and over* was the term she used. You'd think she enjoyed the misery on these men's faces, especially when they begged to own her.

Men are possessive creatures. They like to own things, especially if it serves them beyond their expectations. But Lisa wasn't one to be owned, which is why she made it her goal to fuck Nick and feed on his misery after he came back for more. Call it payback. Call it what you want. Her pride was hurt, and she was frustrated. Being dressed to impress and not getting attention was not making things better.

Nick raised a brow to ask, "Coffee? I already had one earlier."

"Oh, I didn't know," Lisa feigned ignorance. "Another cup won't hurt, would it? You down at least four cups a day, don't you? Too much caffeine for your system. But anything that makes you an outstanding detective, right?"

It was a feeble attempt to get attention. Nick didn't respond, hitting his ballpoint pen on the table at a constant rhythm. This only made her more needy and frustrated.

"I'll just leave it here. You're not going to leave it cold as you do, are you?" Lisa winked.

Nick smirked. Still, no response.

"I'll leave now. See you at lunch, no?" Lisa asked, heading for her office. "Don't-

Nick stood behind her, tracing his fingers through her arm. "I don't leave things cold, Lisa. I leave things warm with a warning." He spoke softly, causing Lisa to stiffen.

And just like that, almost instantly, Lisa was relieved of her frustration and let out an uncontrollable sigh. As if his attention immediately made her go from frustrated and needy to feeling submissive and wanted. Maybe she was like that already and her attitude was just camouflage.

"Yes, sir, you did," Lisa muttered. Those were not the words she had rehearsed in her mind over and over this morning. Her pretty ego was bruised, but the little girl inside her couldn't say anything but that. She had never been turned down her entire life, but this didn't feel like rejection: it felt more like comforting words.

"Oh, don't be stubborn, I could tell it was fake all along. I also see that you wore the best dress to impress. Listen, little girl, one of these two will happen: you'll either pull back from fear, or you'll come back for more of what you don't need. Don't say you weren't warned."

"I think I wore my big girl underwear today, I don't really need your advice," she said, trying to fake her confidence with the situation.

"Your confidence is cute, and I'm sure if I looked, I'd say you were barely wearing any underwear at all," Nick smiled. And as if he knew she was his to do as he pleased, he lifted the dress and displayed her lacy thong front, visibly wet on the bottom as it rode just inside her lips. And as if he were inspecting her, he turned her to see her ass on full display, the only proof the thong was there was where it left the top of the crack of her ass and hugged her waist.

"See, I'm right." At that moment, he struck her ass at about half strength of his muscular arm. "Now like I said, I warned you."

As Nick dropped her dress, Nick sat back down, trying to hide his erection and putting focus back on the case. Lisa, embarrassed and dripping wet, stood there for a moment, attempting to catch her breath. When she did, she rushed out of the door, not knowing how to take in the moment.

"Who the fuck does he think he is?" Lisa said out loud to herself. *He fucking spanked me. And not in a sexual, playful way. Almost like I was being spanked for being bad by a school principal.*

***

Allen stared at the building again, reading the sign one more time. "Star Behavioral Health Group," he mumbled, walking up to the entrance. When he tracked the suspect to California, he had been amused to note he hitched a fight to Fresno. *A wonderful chance to explore Yosemite National Park,* he told himself.

With an address to visit, he had packed light and touched down at Yosemite International Airport at noon. He had found his way to the Kings Canyon road, only to find a place he had never heard of. Pushing his wavy hair out of his eyes, he walked in with a confident stride. The air inside the building was slightly cool and comfortable. He made for the lady dressed in a red polo shirt and tan khakis, standing by the reception area. Behind her was well placed and inviting podium.

She smiled when she saw him, and her eyes roamed his figure, sizing him up and checking if he needed treatment perhaps. That's the same thing Allen would have done if he worked there, although he had hoped his appearance would cause more understanding. His black Oxfords gleamed under the light of the fluorescent bulbs. His suit jacket had been left unbuttoned, revealing a crispy white shirt tucked into tapered navy-blue trousers held up with a black belt with shiny buckle. With his hair framing his face and his wire-rimmed glasses, he had the look of a deranged person of importance. A professor maybe.

"Good day, Sir," she said, "Welcome to Star Behavioral Health Group. What can we do for you today? We offer residential treatment plans for –"

"I'm looking for someone," Allen cut in, saving her the courtesy of finishing whatever monotonous, repetitive line she had been trained to say. "A Mr. Jamal Peters," he said as he rested his palms on her podium, keeping his eyes and smile welcoming.

She paused and the smile on her lips faded and said, "Excuse me?" She blinked.

"I'm in search of Jamal Peters." He tried not to sigh. "He checked in here last week and has not been seen anywhere else since. I'm assuming he's still here?" His face slightly tilted as if asking a question while confident he knew the answer.

She gave him that smile again like she was trying to comprehend his question but was clearly trained in staying delightful in front of customers. "Alright, give me a minute." She raised a finger to him, but her eyes were fixed on the screen in front of her. "I'm sorry but there is no such person here."

"You've got to be kidding me," he said, letting out an audible groan. "Jamal Peters isn't here?" he asked again. There was no way he had been wrong. The mood in the center was semi-formal enough, Allen rested his elbows on the podium as if to get closer and more inviting but instill his will on the situation.

The lady eyed his arms but made no objection. "We have no Jamal Peters here, Sir. Only Niklaus Peters." *Niklaus… maybe, just maybe…*

"Can I speak with Mr. Niklaus then?"

"I'm afraid that's not possible." She shook her head at the computer at replied, "He isn't attending to visitors."

Allen narrowed his eyes at her indifference. Taking off his glasses, he pinched the bridge of his nose with a sigh and spoke, "Mr. Jamal… Niklaus Peters is a suspect in a mass murder in Praxton, Las Vegas." His voice low and calm but his smile was cold and his eyes were hollow. Just as Nick had taught him. "Now if you wish to harbor a potential murder, that's fine with me. Be prepared for a world of lawsuits and arrests. I'm just here to talk to him and save you a lot of hassle." The lady gasped at his threat, raising a hand to her chest, but Allen's demeanor meant her no harm today and she knew it.

Allen continued, "You don't want that. Look up the recent murders in Las Vegas, it's all over the news and I was hired to help solve it." He pushed his acting up and gave her a slow, sadistic smile but remained still as if to say he's going whether she likes it or not. "But, if you let me speak with him, I can ascertain if he's really a murderer and get him off your hands. Or…"

"Okay." The consent came a whimper. "Just… sit over there. I'll… I need to speak with his doctor." She looked as confused as she sounded. With clumsy movements, she picked up the telephone. Allen was smiling brightly now. He nodded at her, and she almost dropped the telephone. *What would Nick give to see me in action,* he mused and went to the white seats by the large windows.

The visitation room reminded him of a small meeting room. There were a couple of seats accompanied by tables arranged in rows. The window with a bed of sweet-smelling and colorful flowers below overlooked the parking lot. He liked the comfort the flowers provided, not only to this meeting but for patients and visitors in general. And there he sat face to face with Niklaus Peters. He matched the photo of Jamal Peters.

He was a brown-skinned man with a heavy-set brow and thick lips. He beamed a bored yet creepy smile like he was watching a comedy show with Allen as the lead. Allen watched him sit and raise one flip-flop-clad foot to the seat so he could rest his hands on his knee.

"They said you wanted to see me." His voice was musical and beautiful, but it was his calculative blue eyes that drew Allen in. That and his black, curly short hair. It was unruly enough to cover his eyes if he dropped his head. It made you want to touch and push it away.

Allen cleared his throat and sat up straighter. "I did, Mr. Peters. Niklaus Peters?"

"Yes," Niklaus answered with a sigh.

"Or should I call you Mr. Jamal Peters?"

"Shhhh," chuckled Jamal. "Don't let them hear you. Jamal lives in Las Vegas. Niklaus lives here."

So he is Jamal, thought Allen, *and Niklaus?* "We will just stick with Mr. Peters if you cooperate. Mr. Peters, are you familiar with a woman, Phoebe Gerald. Small figure, brown hair, doe-eyed?"

"Maybe," He was back to his bored response. "There are many Phoebe Geralds out there. I know more than one–"

"The one you dated," retorted Allen, not putting up with his bullshit. He was finding Jamal's attitude confusing and irritating, but now he knew what type of person he was dealing with.

"Oh, that Phoebe," Jamal smirked, raising his hands from his knee, resting his elbows so he could rest his face on his chin, giving the impression he was bored with this conversation already. "How is she?"

"She's dead." Allen deadpanned. "Two days after you mysteriously disappear only to end up days after her death in a mental asylum."

"Phoebe? Dead? What?" He gasped. His hands were going from resting his chin to covering his mouth while his eyes began glistening with tears that never fell.

"Yes," replied Allen, amused by his sadness. Perhaps it was time to cut to the chase. "Shot alongside her boyfriend, Alex Finnigan, also dead."

Jamal looked up at Allen with a scowl at the mention of the boyfriend. "That's good to know. Almost heartwarming to hear he's gone... but my Phoebe's gone too." He let out a tearful moan, so loudly that the reception lady threw them a concerned look.

Allen smiled at her with a shrug then said to Jamal in a low voice, much like the one he used on the lady, "I don't care for much for theatrics, and I think you are truly mentally unstable. But I'll have you know, Mr. Niklaus Jamal Peters, that you are a prime suspect in the murder of Phoebe Gerald, who was with child,"

"Phoebe was... pregnant?" he whispered the question to himself.

"Yes. She's gone now, alongside Alex Finnigan. So, I hope this place gives you your wits back, but even if it doesn't, it won't stop justice."

Allen rose to his feet, certain of his conclusion. "If you're clean, I suggest an alibi–a good one. If you're not, the next time we'll be meeting would be in Las Vegas. Do have a wonderful day, Mr. Peters. It was nice meeting you."

Allen thanked the lady and walked out of the center with a smirk. *Nick is going to love this.*

Chapter Six.

All was still except for the mechanical whirring of the air conditioning system and the rapid rotations made by the slightly unbalanced ceiling fan. Sunshine from the open windows filled the room with brightness along with a wave of heat the old windows could not hold back. There was the obvious smell of sweaty men mixed with the sweet scent of one of Lisa's latest endeavors.

Allen was sprawled on the couch, clad in cargo shorts and a grey tee shirt. His glasses caught the light that shone from his laptop, masking his eyes as they moved from the screen occasionally to look at Nick, seated on a chair by the window.

Nick sported camo shorts and a black vee-neck shirt that revealed the contours of his toned muscles. His hair was a mess as he ran his hands through it repeatedly as he often did when I was concerned. His look of disgust deepened with each minute, forcing Allen to sigh.

"Can we pretend we have headway in this?" asked Allen, pushing his laptop off his legs.

"No, we cannot," Nick grumbled. It sounded more like a pout to Allen, but he wasn't going to point that out.

"Oh, c'mon," laughed Allen. "It's not that they called the police on you. It was just a…"

"A what, Al?" snapped Nick, turning his stormy eyes on Allen. "They fucking reported a harassment crime. I was this close…this close to getting a restraining order." He used his thumb and index finger to further explain the situation.

"And that's when you played your 'friends with the police' card." Allen cocked his head, amused by Nick's distress. He wasn't in any real trouble; it was the sting on his ego that haunted him.

"It's a good thing you milked every minute to get the info you could 'cause I don't know where to start looking in these files," Allen said as he and Nick pulled their laptops closer and began simultaneously scrolling down on the mouse. "You're the one who's looking. We know of Jamal–"

"Your psychotic pretty boy namesake," quipped Nick, taking his eyes off the screen momentarily.

"Yes, Nicklaus, Jamal, who gives a fuck?" Allen replied as a retort to Nick's sarcastic comment.

"We sectioned the killings into three groups based on injury patterns," Nick continued as if to ignore Allen's comment. "We've got him transferred to a center here for easy questioning. We figured the murders weren't all at Praxton. We're on the trail for where Phoebe and Alex were last seen. We figured all of this out by spending hours on those files."

"No," Allen countered, lifting his gaze to Nick as if to go toe to toe with sarcasm. "I have spent hours on them, you didn't, but together, we figured it out."

"Hey." Nick cracked a smile, realizing this now became a who has the bigger sarcastic dick contest. "I spent hours with the family members of the victims."

"Harassing them, I'm sure," Allen laughed, taking advantage of the moment to push Nick's buttons.

"Maybe I should have–" A voice screamed from the streets pulling Nick's attention. It ended as quickly as it started, and all was still again. Allen pushed his laptop aside and rose to his feet.

"What in the world was that?" He stretched his arms.

"Always with the questions," Nick smirked.

"It's what I do–" Another scream punctuated the air. This time it didn't stop. It continued as mindless rambling. At least that's what Allen could make of it.

"Never a dull moment in Praxton, eh," Nick chuckled and rose to his feet. He was moving to the door before Allen had time to reply.

Nick whistled and called Allen to come over. The recognition was instant. *The boy at the jewelry store!* He was standing there on the sidewalk, looking rather pale. His blue shirt was dusty and his jeans were stained with a brown smear that looked a lot like mud. It wasn't his attire that startled Allen but the wild look in his eyes and the shaky hand that held a shiny handgun, which Nick could see was a Glock.

The street filled with spectators as others heard the commotion the boy was making. Some people stood behind windows while others stood behind doors and peeked around them, but nobody made a move to soothe the boy. He stood there, breathing heavily and watching the increasing crowd.

He stiffened when he locked eyes with them. In the next instant, he held the Glock to his head. Nick moved first but the blast of a gun stopped him in his tracks. Allen saw a breath of relief leave the boy before his eyes squinted shut and then open just before he pulled the trigger. Then came the blood and screams; the boy's eyes remained open and empty, but with a sense of peace that nobody else felt.

A moment of compassion and grief immediately entered Nick as he had wanted to save the boy, but he couldn't. The man who had once calmed the boy felt helpless. Allen remained back but was equally as distraught as he watched the events unfold. They both locked eyes: they had to figure this out, and quickly.

***

Nick watched the sky as the clouds gathered, blocking the rays of the sun and giving small relief to the blazing heat. A glance at his watch and a quiet sigh escaped his lips. "Just rain already!" *Anything to wash the blood and off the curb.*

He closed his eyes and the boy's as if to say a prayer with a goodbye and last respects. *Eyes as blue as mine.* When his eyes opened, he saw Allen giving his account to the police. He knew the standard questions and had no taste to answer any at the moment. He remembered the boy from the jewelry store robbery. He had saved him when he was nowhere in sight but failed him when he only moments away.

He raised a hand to his hair, moving his fingers softly through it as he usually did when he felt helpless and angry. With a heave of air, he stepped back into his office. *Never a dull moment in Paxton.* He almost wished he didn't live in the apartment upstairs. Not when his window gave him a perfect view of a suicide scene. Normally things didn't bother him at this level, but this was personal. He felt like the boy's guardian and almost responsible, even though he kept telling himself otherwise.

Avoiding his room, he bounded up the stairs and took a right for the gym. When returning downstairs, the sun had begun its descent and Lisa was back. She was wrapped in a short yellow sundress that left her shoulders bare. The dress was held up by a scrap of a sleeve he could easily slide off as it appeared too loose for her frame. Her hair was bunched high on her head in a bun with some stray strands framing her face.

Reminding himself of reality, he focused on Allen as he recounted the event that occurred in Lisa's absence. She smiled as he spoke. Nick's eyes narrowed when she placed a hand on Allen's arm, apologizing that he had to see that. Allen reminded her that he had seen things like this all the time, but that didn't make it any better for him or Nick. It only calmed her that they would be okay.

Allen reminded Lisa of a concerned friend, always trying to take care of her even if he had to lie about his discomfort to get there. He was gentle and nice, always understanding. Lisa thought it would be Allen and not Nick she would go to if she ever had to cry over a guy. It would also be Allen if she ever needed to cuddle, although she shook her head as that thought crossed her mind.

Screw this, Nick said under his breath as he took a big step on the stairs. Allen and Lisa broke the their sweet gaze and turned at the noise.

"Hello, Mr. Stone," Lisa said with a squinty glance and bubbly smile. He gave her a tight-lipped smile and answered with a grunt.

"What have you been up to?" asked Allen, stepping away from Lisa.

Nick said nothing, letting the sweat glistening on his bare arms and face do the talking.

"Never mind," Allen said and dropped to the nearest couch. Lisa remained standing with a stack of papers pressed to her chest.

Nick stared at the contours of her collarbone and the soft rise and fall of her firm breasts, pushing out the stack of papers she held against her. *Focus, Nick,* he groaned and walked away. In the mini kitchen, he grabbed a bottle of water and drank it, followed by a moan of relief. His first question when he returned to the room was to Lisa. She was still standing by the couch, while Allen sat resting his head.

"What's that?" He pointed to the papers.

"Oh, this!" Lisa held out the stack, relieving her chest of them.

Allen opened his eyes at the question and closed them again. "I sent Lisa to retrieve the crime records from the station."

"And this couldn't be sent through fax or secure email, why?" He moved closer and grabbed one before she stopped them on the coffee table. He flipped through it, standing by the window, and was drawn instead to a young man walking by across the street. He paused and watched the police clean up the scene.

File closed. Suicide. He groaned and focused on the boy.

"Isn't that Jose?" he called Allen.

The rustling of the couch announced Allen's reply. "Bernie's friend?"

"Yeah," Nick answered, moving closer for a better view. "Is there something different about him?"

"Different how?" Allen's fancy for asking questions was turned on high.

"Just different." He had watched the boy observe the scenes and move on. His shoes were white, he had visited the barbershop, and his clothes looked clean and new. The last time Nick had seen him was two days ago at the gas station where he sometimes worked. He looked as unkept as he always did; but now, he looked clean cut and professional.

"Out on a date, maybe," Allen quipped. "You can't impress a girl looking like trash, can you?"

"What a girl that must be," Nick mused and turned to Lisa. "It's getting late. Shouldn't your bedtime be coming up?"

"Oh!" She blinked and brushed the hair off her face, not responding to his sarcasm. "Yes… of course." She rushed behind her desk and retrieved a scrap of paper, gathered her purse and books into her back tote bag. She hurried past Nick and entered the kitchen. The sound of running water wafted out.

"Would you slow down," Allen laughed, rising to his feet. "No one's on your tail with a gun."

The water stopped and she returned with her bag on her shoulder. "Some days I forget someone lives in the building and end up being a nuisance late into the evening."

If she meant the kind of nuisance he had witnessed the other night, then Nick was welcome to it. Allen also didn't mind her walking away slowly as he enjoyed how the loose sundress slightly revealed her shapely ass. He was less of a tight skirt kind of guy and more into a comfortable sundress or blue jeans. Nick wanted to leave nothing to the imagination with a full face of makeup and perfectly placed hair, where Allen liked his women to feel comfortable in their clothing, no makeup and a messy bun. Today was Allen's day to feed his desires, but that didn't stop Nick from wondering what was underneath.

She walked past Allen and picked up the papers. "I really must get going though. I'll have these sorted out by tomorrow."

"Hey, hold up," Allen shook his head with a sigh. "Pause… breathe. No one's forcing you to hurry."

Allen didn't physically put his arm around her, but his words made her feel like he did.

Nick swallowed his comment, choosing to drop the paper in his hand on her stack. "Yeah, Ms. Monroe, no one's pressing you to hurry up." His grin said otherwise.

"But.." Allen put his hand to the small of her back. "We understand you need to be elsewhere." She smiled at his understanding and calming tone and walked toward the door. "Go home, rest up," Allen continued after stifling a yawn, "and we will see you tomorrow."

"Okay," smiled Lisa. Nick watched the sun's last rays make her skin golden and wished she would stay a nuisance and that Allen would stop touching her so freely.

"Good night." She gave them both a little awkward wave and smiled as she felt eyes on her ass as she walked out.

Nick turned his eagle's gaze for a second to watch Allen return to his couch when a scream pierced the air for the second time that day. His heart almost fell to his stomach when he saw the men colliding with Lisa. Just a few men accidentally running into Lisa as she hit the sidewalk. Although they were very apologetic, they didn't know how close they were to Allen and Nick wanting to break their jaw. Instead, Allen and Nick helped her up and on here way. As they re-entered the office, they both sat down, looked at each other, and could tell what each other was thinking.

For once, can we just have a dull moment in Praxton?!

Chapter Seven.

"You know they blame us for what happened the other day?" Nick said to Allen huskily, almost unbothered.

"They blame us for everything. Not *us, us.* You. You have amassed quite the list of enemies, Nick. Enemies everywhere. Sadly, this time I'm in this too."

"You should exonerate yourself. I'm okay with being a bad guy. And a lazy detective."

Allen laughed loudly, filling the air with his laughter.

"At least one of us can still laugh, right?" Nick tried to say with a grin.

"I like how unphased you are, Nick. These are the things that make you a good detective. I know we're going to find out. It's just taking longer, but it's not something we can't pull off."

"Enough with the pep talk, Allen. I might mistake you for Lisa."

Another loud laughter.

"Speaking of Lisa, how is she? Poor girl," Nick asked with concern.

"Lisa might seem small and fragile, but she's quite strong. She's seen things in life - that's what I think, at least," Allen replied, not certain of the answer he just gave. More of an educated guess based on his interactions.

"How is she handling everything?"

"She's doing better than you expect, really," Allen continued, "given the circumstance."

"That's good, then," Nick sighed, "Do you think she has personal problems she hasn't been upfront about? Money issues?"

"I haven't noticed. What makes you think so?"

"She shows signs. Maybe I'm overthinking it. I spotted another homeless person yesterday. I'm almost losing count. These things bother me. I really don't like not knowing and not being able to help out if I could."

"I might have noticed too, but don't you think profiling your coworker is wrong? And Lisa is a sweet, sweet girl, so why should we ruin that?" Allen said, repeating sweet as if to coddle her even though she wasn't there.

"I'm just doing my work as a detective, Allen. Don't be such a sap."

"Let's be careful not to lose people in the process, Nick."

Nick threw a glance at him. He could sense the concern and denial in Allen's voice. Was it the homeless person or Lisa? "We have a deadline to beat, remember? Let's work towards that."

Nick tried to change the topic. He was concerned and bothered at the same time. What bothered him was torn between Lisa and the homeless person, just like Allen. This work had taken more of a toll than it should have.

Nick hardly doubted his capacity, but this was almost driving him insane. What's the missing piece? But this time, it wasn't just one piece missing. All fragments of the case were missing, and the more they dug, the more confusing it got. Nick prided in his job. A lot. Half his lifetime, success, and achievement were all tied to his being a successful Detective. Nick was dying to bundle these pieces and get this over with.

Lisa walked into the room, interrupting the boys' bonding time, carrying customized coffee as usual.

"I got coffee!" she said, placing each person's cup on their table. The cups had their names on them. "Yeah, I had your names written on the cup. I had exchanged cups with Nick the other morning and I almost lost it. I'm sure you guys thought I must've gone crazy with all that energy I displayed." She laughed.

Allen followed.

Nick smiled.

"Big day today, right?" she asked, placing Allen's cup on his table. "You're open to anything. It's Cappuccino this morning."

"That's thoughtful of you. I might learn to stick to one someday," he laughed.

"I think it's cute that you're open to anything," she said, flashing a Hallmark movie worthy smile.

"Maybe we should get a fancier coffee machine for the office?" Nick butted in with obvious jealousy in his tone.

"Sounds great!" Lisa jumped, as if Amazon.com was her next stop.

"Nice one. Considering that we might be working overtime to conclude this shit, we need all the help we can," Allen said, adding his two cents.

"You make coffee sound like crack," Lisa interrupted.

"Well, isn't it? What else can you do to make Nick our golden Detective?" Allen said with quite the smirk.

They all exchanged smiles, with Nick's and Allen's obvious as to the intent of the statement. Lisa also smiled but turned her face and moved her hair as if to hide her slightly flushed grin. It was her intent to be shy and innocent to the sexual inuendo. But Allen and Nick saw right through it, feeling accomplished at teaming up and making her blush.

"We have work, and a long day too," Nick said, sharing a glance at Lisa who pretended not to see him.

"Yes. Lisa, today we're staying with you. We've been trying to get little work done before you came in. Your station is quite messed up. Don't freak out yet, but we plan on fixing it soon… before Halloween if the case permits us to do it ourselves."

"Thank you so much. Maybe we could have dinner together. My treat?" she said with wide eyes, not hiding her joy at the thought of taking care of them.

Nick looked up. He could tell she was sincere. Not because of the tears that had welled up in her eyes at the thought of having company for dinner, but her reaction to them accepting. Nick paid more attention to body language than he did to people's words. *How is she so soft, yet so fierce sexually?* Nick thought.

"If we're doing that, we might as well get to it." Nick stood, shuffling papers on his worktable.

"Oh, yes, we should." Allen followed.

"Thank you so much." Lisa let out softly.

***

The next day, Allen left early to pick up his niece from school. It was becoming a routine. Lisa and Nick were wrapping up with the day's work when the phone rang for the second time in a row, but no one answered. Lisa had arrived to work that day with a tighter dress and a cockier attitude from the day before. She did not intend to test Nick's patience, but she did. She flaunted it and he noticed.

"Didn't I warn you" Nick said, "about me?"

"How… Wait, did I do something wrong?" she replied, visibly fumbling her words.

"You think because you made us dinner that you can walk around here like you own the place and have us feeding out of your hands? Allen isn't here to save your smart ass."

"Maybe I don't want Allen to save my ass," she said, almost daring him to spank her again by sticking it out slightly.

Nick stared at her, unable to hide his joy at seeing it. "How long have you known that me doing that to you turned me on and I haven't been able to stop thinking about it?"

"I feel your eyes on my ass every time I walk away," she responded, "and you don't really hide that you stare at my tits when I'm coming toward you."

"You think you're playing me like the boys your age?" Nick smirked. "Just because you know how to work the boys doesn't mean you can control the man. And I am the man."

"You're the one thinking of me every night when you go upstairs," she said with a lip biting grin and eyes practically begging for attention.

"You learn quickly. Are you using my tricks against me? I don't play games: I am the game. And when you lose my game, you get spanked, and know I don't always use just my hand."

Lisa's bodily response shocked him even more. She was unphased and remained too calm for someone who had been threatened to be punished.

Nick smiled. *She didn't know. Not a smart move.*

"Should I cry 'Daddy', 'Uncle', or 'Master' while you try?" She arched her brow mockingly, attempting to sarcastically dare him.

"It doesn't matter what you cry, only that you do," he responded, his gaze as cold as his last name.

Oh shit, what did I just do? "I need a drink of water," Lisa said, walking to the water dispenser at the other corner of her office. She filled the paper cup and gulped down water as if her life depended upon it. It turned Nick on, especially the fact that he was teasing her, and it was working. He liked her mouthiness in this moment. Almost like a brat that begged to be tamed.

"Would you like some?" she asked.

"I'll come get it myself. You seem a little flushed right now. You keep drinking."

"Is that why you turn me on and turn me away because I don't run from you or because I welcome it?" Lisa needed an answer.

"Damn you," Nick groaned. "God fucking damn you, Lisa. Was this your idea? Push me past my breaking point to see who I really am?"

Without even realizing it, he pressed his lips against hers, pulling her by the hips and pinning her to the wall. He placed her perfectly, where he could access every part of her body, without her repulsion. She dared not move at all. He manhandled her, and his muscles were tense. She could resist or try and move, but it wouldn't matter. He had her where he wanted her.

Desperation fueled the kiss. She was more than welcoming; she kissed back with the same neediness.

How had they managed to stay the same with the level of heat growing between them at just a kiss was a mystery. Nick could feel her struggle to maintain her balance while running her hands through his hair. He lifted her, making her wrap her legs around his waist, not breaking loose from the kiss.

"Open for me, Lisa. Right now." His dominant voice seared her skin, dampening her panties even more.

She wrapped her legs around his lean hips even tighter as her dress slid up around her hips and his bulge pressed against her, sending friction against her clit. Demanding impulses of intense pleasure ran throughout her body. She knew that a climax was only seconds away. Some of it was his cock physically rubbing her clit, but there was no doubt she was on the brink from him speaking dominant words in his dominant tone.

His lips devoured hers, slanting against them as his tongue fed from her. They both met the kiss with a greater demand of their own. The aching arousal was like an animal clawing at them both, making it difficult for one to let go of the other.

This wasn't just some ego-soothing game for Lisa; this she knew. Nick was fucking hot, and every woman with a vagina drooled over him. It took his groin intensely slamming against her wet pussy to realize he wasn't just eye candy.

"Please don't stop, I'm begging you," she said in a pant. He didn't need to do too much for her to climax as his words and intense kissing already had her close. She had created several images of them fucking over and over in her head and this was merely a finishing touch. Lisa had longed for this. "I'm almost there," she cried.

Nick didn't stop, and this time he didn't want to. He let out a groan as his lips pulled away from hers. He held her against the wall with one hand as his other one pulled from her thighs and toward her top. He pulled her dress down, practically ripping it and pulled the bra over her tits, exposing her nipples. He was determined that she have an orgasm without fucking her, just to show her he had that level of control.

When his lips surrounded one rock hard nipple, Lisa let out an incoherent gasp, dragging her across the wall uncontrollably. He wasn't gentle, and she didn't want him to be. She needed this - to be manhandled by him. His teeth gipped her sensitive nipple, periodically going from slightly biting to sucking.

"Oh, fuck, I'm almost there. Please, Nick, don't stop," she cried.

"Please what?" he asked, momentarily removing his mouth, still holding her still but staring into her eyes.

"Please sir, please Daddy, please Master, please anything you fucking want, just please don't stop!" she replied with a whimpering yet submissive tone. She was really begging. This game had become real now as she would have done anything in this moment to cum.

"Not yet, Lisa," he said when he felt her shudder, almost jerking as he placed his mouth on her other breast.

"Come here you little slut." He loosened her thighs, forcing her to lower her legs to the floor, despite her whimper, and went to his knees before her. Normally she wouldn't like being called a slut, but in this moment as it escaped his lips, that was exactly what she was, and they both knew it.

"Yes sir," she said, doing exactly what he asked.

"Take your panties off and hand them to me," he said, eye level with her pussy but looking into her eyes.

Fumbling to obey, she pulled them off as fast as she could and handed them to him. They were soaked, practically dripping. He stood up with them and placed them in her mouth. Confused but not caring what he did to her, she accepted them. She tasted her own wetness for the first time in her life. Normally this wouldn't turn her on, but in this moment Nick could do anything he wanted and it would turn her on. She then felt her legs forced as wide as they could be standing against a wall.

He first placed his fingers to feel how wet she was, her bare mound glistening. "What a beautiful pussy," he moaned, as he placed his lips on hers until they were opening up.

His tongue lapped the soft skin. He moaned when he tasted how wet she was, showing her desire for him. His fingers spread her soft folds as his tongue found her needy clit. *Oh, God, Nick.*

Her writhing cry filled his senses as the soft, sweet taste of her exploded against his tongue and the tight, hot grip of her sex began to surround his questing fingers. She was so wet that she dripped down her leg. He began to fondle inside her, drenched with her wetness. "I want you to cum for me, Lisa," he said against her soft mound. His breath sent shivers all over her.

His lips moved over her clit, catching it in the gentle suction of his mouth as his tongue began to flicker over her. His fingers moved inside her, stretching and filling her before curling his finger and finding the sensitive spot inside, just behind her clit. He rubbed gently as he increased the friction on her clit. Not fast, not slow, just hard enough with perfect rhythm.

He knew that she was close when her body tightened, and her hands tangled in his hair in a pull. Whatever the hell he was doing with his fingers and tongue was destroying her, sending her away to an orgasm she could barely contain. He was rubbing against something that made her clit pulse in warning, swell, and demand relief. She was almost fighting for freedom. The panties muffled her voice and made it hard to breathe through her mouth, but she dared not remove them.

She held on even tighter when the pressure from his mouth increased, the sizzle of impending orgasm rushing along her spine. Her fingers dug into his hair even deeper as he suckled at her clit, harder, faster, with consistent strokes of his index finger giving the "come here" motion on her g-spot. His tongue worked a masterpiece, massaging and teasing the outside while his finger took care of the inside.

She let out a muffled cry as the orgasm slammed through her, jerking her with hard spasms as her sex convulsed around his fingers and tightened almost painfully before releasing again. It was jerking the strength from her legs, leaving her helpless in his grip.

Stars exploded through her head as she finally slumped against the wall. Nick had finally released her after wringing out every ounce of energy. And now she was completely exhausted as she came down from what just took a toll on her body.

"What did I tell you?" he said as she sit there slumped while he licked his fingers clean. He took the panties from her mouth and kept them in his hand. "These are mine now; you won't need them the rest of the day. Go home and rest."

Lisa stood up and straightened up her dress and tried to gather herself. He didn't try to hug or hold her, just took her underwear. Lost in what just happened, she went to the bathroom and shut the door behind her. Very conflicted, she had both the hottest sexual experience she'd ever had, but it lacked the emotional affect needed afterward.

When she came out of the bathroom Nick was again looking at case notes.

"I should go home now," she said, half wanting him to ask her to stay but half needing to be alone to absorb what just happened.

"I'll see you tomorrow," he said, basically ignoring what just happened between them. "Wear something comfortable so Allen doesn't think you're a slut."

What a fucking asshole. She half wanted to chew him out for his response; but as she began walking to the door with her pussy beginning to drip down her leg with no panties to stop it, "Yes sir" was all she could get out.

I told you Lisa, this wouldn't be another cold coffee. I like to finish what I start.

Chapter Eight.

Nick rolled the black SUV into the parking lot, with both hands still on the wheel. He smiled to no one in particular for he was alone. Then Allen's voice broke through the speakers.

"Ultimatums are quite unhealthy."

"I find them rather stimulating," smirked Nick, his sharp blue gaze fell on a red Bugatti gleaming in the sunlight. He liked it for its speed and style. He could afford it too. But the SUV stole his heart with its versatility and humble look.

"Of course you do," laughed Allen, bringing him back to the conversation. "Hopefully, we can figure this thing out before then."

"So optimistic of you." He clicked his seat belt, and the strap unfurled from his body, giving him room to move freely. "To not call it as it is. We have till the weekend, and we barely have anything,"

"A week or a month," quipped Allen. "If we solve this case, time will be of no matter. The police have nothing, and their detectives are dumb as rocks. Well, now they are."

"Such encouraging words." Nick rolled his eyes and reached for his phone and satchel in the passenger's seat, comparing me to rocks."

"You know I try." He could picture Allen in his silver Ashton Martin. The guy was so loved by people that gifts came by the month, but Allen was too modest to flaunt them. "Speaking of deadlines, are you there yet?"

"Yeah," replied Nick. He pushed his greying hair out of his face. "You?"

"Yeah. It looks like the kind of place for a murder."

"Mine doesn't," he said, catching a glimpse of flowers, climbing vines, and a rooftop dining area. "And yet, I have a feeling something happened here."

"Always trust your gut," Allen reminded him. "You've solved most our cases that way."

"My gut tells me to get out of the car, but my brain says drive the hell out of here!"

"Then follow your gut. Your brain and dick always get you in trouble. We'll converge at–"

"Yes, yes, I know," Nick brushed him off. "I don't need a reminder of my day or my dick troubles." He popped the door open, meeting the glare of the sun outside.

"Later." Allen's remark felt like a question. He hummed in agreement and killed the engine.

He was alone again and thought little of it. Stuffing his keys and phone into his pockets, he stepped out into the late morning sun, grateful he had dressed lightly. With tan trousers, a black vintage shirt, and tan Vans, he was ready for a day of talking without appearing to be a nuisance.

He trailed the cream-painted walls and met the entrance after a sharp turn to the right. The building was designed so that the entrance was semi-detached from the main building with a walkway of flowers growing on metal arches connecting them. His eyes lifted to the upstairs area that held billowing cream canopies. *Very fancy. Maybe an early lunch to get the entire feel.*

He walked closer to the short cast iron gate that served as a door and stepped in. The interior was as bright as the exterior with cream paint accentuated with gold metal and green from the plants. The smell of jasmine wafted through the air, and he spotted the cream-colored petals everywhere. *Talk about sticking with a theme.*

Every flower that bloomed was either cream or pale white. He particularly liked the white roses by the reception desk. There was no one in line, so he went straight for the brown-skinned and bright smiled receptionist - not skinny but not overweight, either. She smiled when she noticed him and displayed her big brown eyes. Her hair was adorned with daisies, complemented by teeth as white as snow. He could tell that she believed in good hygiene but didn't perform much exercise. The bare skin of her right shoulder glinted in the light of the room, while the other held the sleeve of her cream dress firmly intact.

"Welcome to The Solar. My name is Rhonda," Her voice was cheery and kind enough so as not to sound forced. "It's a lovely day, isn't it?" He caught a longing in her voice that lasted only seconds. "Perfect for trying out our latest menu, 'Dining with Nature'. It leaves you feeling vitalized and at one with –"

"Let me stop you there, sweetheart." He raised a finger to say, "I'm Detective Nick Stone." He flashed her his badge. "A case of multiple murders was linked to this restaurant" as Rhonda gasped, blinking to restore her focus. "Yeah. I have a permit and everything. So, if you'd be so kind as to answer some questions and lead me to the next person to be questioned, that would be nice."

"Um... yes, I... well what do you want to know?" Rhonda moved from behind the desk to reveal a long cream dress that hugged her figure down to her hips and then flared out in soft waves. It was a dress that many women would wear to hide their figure but also display it at the same time. Nick smirked in approval. "Can we sit? I'll... Can I get you anything?"

She raised a hand to smoothen the edges of her hair and dropped one to her hip. Nick held a chuckle at her reactions. *She's going to be easy.*

"Please sit," she urged him and disappeared into the walkway.

Nick obliged and walked to a beige couch with a low back at the edge of the room with the best view, right next to a vase of pale white roses. *How had they gotten the right shade to suit the cream walls?* Nick thought for a second but realized quickly he could care less. He approved of the restaurant and the setting and that was enough. If ever he went on a date again, this would be a good place.

Rhonda returned, less shaky with a tray of holding wine and a plate of bread. "Mr. Pietro would be with us in a moment," announced Rhonda. "He'd like to hear what you have to say."

Nick gave her a curt smile. *Men and protecting their business from negative news.* "Of course. Shall we begin?" Rhonda nodded, and her lips twitched for a second. *Don't be scared, sweetheart, you have nothing to do with this.*

***

The hallway was a sterile white that reminded Allen of his childhood days at the ophthalmologist. He had feared anything gory or bloody. Even the thought of it made him queasy, but he was grown now and had seen every kind of gory and horrible thing because of his job and his prior life. Besides, it was a place for the dead, not the living. Perhaps that was what made Nick queasy. He sat with his head between his knees on a bench lining the walls and where Allen stood, with arms crossed at the edge of the intersection that led to the morgue.

"Ready?" he asked Nick with a deep exhale.

"Yeah," sighed Nick and raised his head. He ran his hand through his already messy hair. With a few deep breaths, he pushed himself off the bench, straightened his collar, and threw Allen a cocky grin.

Allen shook his head in a chuckle and led the way to the doors. Nick followed closely behind. They both had their reasons for not liking the morgue. The memory of friends who had died right before Nick's eyes haunted him, especially the ones he had tried to save. He was better now, and his episodes were less frequent, but they would never go away and he knew that.

Allen's reason smacked him in the face the moment he passed through the doors. It came like a slow choking smell that starts sweet and ends sour. He was barely five steps in when it turned to a sharp burning sensation on the tip of his nose. His eyes began to water, and he coughed while trying to release the clog forming in his throat.

"Well, look who it is," came a high-pitched voice accented with a southern drawl. It belonged to a woman, the only reason they could find to look forward to a visit to the morgue.

"Anastasia," Nick chuckled. "Am I welcome in your domain?"

"It's Stacie to you. When are you never welcome, Nick?" She appeared from behind a long metal table stripped clean of a body. Her blonde curls were raised in a low ponytail–a hastily made one, no doubt– and her blue eyes shined with a calming sense, even when death controls the room.

"I typically think they don't want me here," Nick said, alluding to the corpses.

"They're afraid you going to wake them up with a kiss of life," she quipped and straightened her navy-blue work coat, "but I'm not."

"I'd be much obliged, Anastasia, but I'm afraid now is not the time," Nick answered.

"It is Stacie. And yes, I was meaning to tell you…" She pulled gloves out of her pocket and wiggled her fingers into them. Reaching for a metal drawer, she stopped. "Up for some time with the dead?"

"No!" Allen said in chorus with Nick, both of them looking like hilarious cowards in unison.

"Pity," she pouted and crossed her arms. "It would have been easier to explain… No matter, you two are brilliant enough." Bending her hand to look like a gun, she placed it above her heart. "We found two things. One, the bullet wound to Phoebe was aimed here. One straight shot to the heart that grazed her hand when she tried to block it. We ran a simulation."

"Okay," Allen nodded with furrowed brows.

"She did so… because…." Stacie bobbed her head forward like she wanted them to complete her statement.

"Because she was shot from a…distance?" Nick thought out loud.

"Yes! Yes! Yes!!" clapped Stacie. "And the man… his bullet wound was identical in location only he had no bullet graze on his hand and was point blank."

"He didn't try to defend himself?" Allen gave Stacie a puzzled look.

"Perhaps, but the front of his chest showed the imprint of the gun barrel and his hand had residue of gunpowder. There were no signs of a struggle that we could find. And the way the body was found… this could only mean,"

"He shot Phoebe, then shot… himself?" Allen was trying to connect the dots.

"Bingo! It does appear she died before he did. So, yes, we have our possible killer."

Chapter Nine

"I got it. I got it! I got it!" Lisa ran into the office, not stopping to breathe. "I got it, guys!"

"Got what?" Allen and Nick asked at the same time

"The ownership certificate… erm, Mr. Bolton, remember?" She seemed calmer now.

Nick and Allen looked too surprised to question her. Seeing the disappointment in her eyes, Nick said, "Wow, that's great. good job. But why did you go all the way?"

"The dead couple both owned guns before they were murdered but the woman sold hers to a friend shortly before the murder. Meanwhile, the man always carried his."

"Impressive, Lisa, quite impressive. " Allen cut Nick off, stopping him from further questioning.

Nick was authoritative but went overboard sometimes. He never minced words. What he believed in mattered more than anything, and he practiced and preached logic. He could be your best friend today but would never hesitate to call you out the moment you derailed.

Nick and Allen were both worried and concerned. Everyone amongst the three of them had their various job descriptions. They had their roles appointed to them, which they followed judiciously. Lisa could seem quiet, but she never seemed like a pushover. She was never one to people please, and never failed to speak up. She didn't do this to impress them, and Nick knew it very well. She didn't even do it to impress anyone. *So, why did she?*

Allen had questions too but wouldn't ask. He had grown so soft before the case. Stopped working extra hours, cut back on coffee, went home immediately after work hours. He had a work car he used to run errands. He caught bad guys but went out of his way, so they didn't trace him back to his house or extended family.

Nick's worries were different. He lived right above the office, stayed extra hours, and overworked himself to see that every case was concluded. He fancied himself and fancied the women he was with. Of course, that is until he fucked them. Then they were yesterday's news.

"I had gotten a lead and decided to follow through to the end," Lisa said, with her head lifted.

"Followed a lead without us?" Nick asked, his eyes bloodshot from the lack of sleep, his tone serious and deep.

Why is he this mad? Lisa wondered to herself. *I thought he would be proud of me.*

"You took quite a risk. What if you had gotten hurt?" Allen asked sincerely, looking concerned.

She had known both enough to expect Nick to be the asshole and Allen to be soft and gentle. But both were concerned in their own way, and that made her smile. "I was careful. I watched my back. Crossed every T and never crossed a place twice. And look what it brought us. At least we have another lead."

"Yeah. This is a big one. A big break." Allen said.

"You did well. Any other updates so far? Apart from the one we know? Nick said with a half grin.

"No. None at all."

"You can go now." She was dismissed. She walked to the door of the reception area and stood there.

"We have so much work to do today," Allen said. "Work that might require us to stay extra hours. I'll work extra during lunch break to make up because I'll leave after work. Is that okay?" Allen asked.

"That's not a problem. The technicians would be here at exactly five. Lisa and I would have to go elsewhere to work while they fix things." Nick answered.

"What are they fixing?" Lisa asked, crossing her arms over her chest.

"The coffee maker and TV. The TV in your office is broken too." Nick sighed.

"Oh, wow. I didn't expect you to take it seriously the day I mentioned it."

"Well, speak for yourself, Lisa. I've known Nick for a long time. Anyone who stays with him knows he'd pull through anything. Anything at all." Allen shrugged, pushing his glasses up his nose.

Why am I not surprised? Lisa looked at Nick, expecting feedback, but he didn't flinch.

You shouldn't. He's your boss.

"That's okay, guys. Let's get to work." Nick dismissed the two of them.

***

"What did you do that for?" Lisa asked.

"Do what?"

"Don't play dumb," she said with a concerned look.

"Mind the words you use, you're in my house."

They had decided to settle for Nick's apartment upstairs to be close to the technicians just in case they needed anything.

"But you're playing a dumb asshole," she said in defiance to his gaze.

"One more word from you and you'll be weak in the knees."

"I'm not scared," she said, knowing that the last time they were this intense, she had the best orgasm of her life. She also had the heavy weight on her that he didn't display emotion after her orgasm, and she was dead set to fix it.

Lisa stared at Nick as if to dare him, knowing it would push his buttons.

Lust sizzled in Nick's groin, torturing his erection and tightening it further. He swore he was harder than he had ever been in his life. "Come closer. Just one step bitch."

"I don't like that word and I don't appreciate you calling me that," Lisa replied, not moving a muscle. Her defiance was short lived as she moved one step in his direction with a smirk on her face.

"I think you know where this ends, but you push me anyway?" he said, almost asking her to keep going.

Lisa stood taller, the dress she wore tightening to her body. She was Nick's type. Tiny in the waist, handful sized boobs with wide hips holding her luscious ass in place. Nick had fantasized about giving those round butts brutal backstroke with a paddle and belt. He had threatened it.

"Why do you act like you've not licked me? I haven't stopped thinking about it, Nick."

She had taken more than a step, but it was more than enough. She had removed her jacket, showing off her slender shoulders, and she had let down her hair. Her gaze hit the floor as she tried to keep eye contact, but it wasn't enough. Her defiance was short lived, and she knew she was under his control no matter the fight.

"Come over here and tell me all about it." Nick said as he used his index finger displaying the 'come here' gesture.

"I won't. You'll beg for me this time."

Nick smiled, "You have no idea what you are getting into. We can play bratty games and I can punish you or you can do as you are told and come over here."

"I think I do," Lisa said, standing just where Nick sat, tracing her fingers from his neck to his arm. "I know exactly what you can do, and I've experienced it."

Nick didn't move, just looked up at her and smiled. Lisa bent even further to whisper into his ears when he grabbed her by the hips, sitting her on his lap and planting his lips on hers. He had wanted to do that the moment she had run into the office this morning.

"One more word from you, and I'll spank your ass. So, I suggest you sit there and be a good girl."

"Yes, you've threated that before, " Lisa said with a huge smile, almost as if she won this round, "But you never came through."

That was the wrong thing to say to Nick. A trigger, calling him out as less than a man because he promised a spanking and only gave her an orgasm. The bitch needed to learn now.

He kissed her, almost softly, luring her into thinking she had won. She kissed back, almost hugging him for how gentle he was being. She craved dominance but she craved soft emotion just as much and was almost gushing from Nick being like this. And just like that, he broke the kiss, standing up to loosen his tie, and tossing it to the desk. Lisa was panting. She rolled the dress off her skin, then made to reach for him, grabbing him impatiently. He swatted her hand away.

"Oh, no, this isn't how you decide." Nick drove her to the wall, pressing her against it while leaning back to grab her wrists, shackling them over her head to a pre-placed restraint that kept her upright. "I'm the one in control here."

His hands were like hydraulic jacks on her wrists, impossible to move. It was hard to maintain eye contact when she could feel her wetness dripping between her thighs but couldn't move her hands to resist. She had taken the spanking threat to heart and now her inability to move had given her the reality that she had no control. Her vagina convulsed heavily as her eyes filled with fear. She looked up at the restraints, wondering if they were placed there for her or been there all along.

"Why are you doing this to me?" she cried with her hands tugging at the shackled restraints.

"I'm going to show you exactly why I hadn't taken you there at the office the other day. Now, ask me to remove your panties and bra," he ordered.

He was nothing like she had imagined. She had expected something close, but not like this. She liked his dominance, but she was a little scared. It was nothing like she'd known.

"No, I don't want to," she responded with a pouty face, still trying to tug her hands out of the restraints. "Let me go!"

"Are you scared little girl?"

"A little, yes."

"I warned you and you pushed me."

"It's… my first time, I didn't know it would get this far," Lisa defended, finally stopping her resistance and standing still.

"I could stop here. I won't go any farther and I will let you go. But now you know what I am. This is your choice," he said, backing away from her and giving her time to think.

"Sounds like you're a coward. I dared you, remember?" she responded. *What the fuck did I just say?* Seeing the intensity of the hunger and emotion in his eyes, she knew that she'd never be the same again after this. His smile as he reached for her proved it, but Lisa didn't mind. She'd come a long way to back out.

"I've never been spanked and punished like this," she said in an utterly sensual manner.

"Well, there's always a first time. I'll go easy on you." Nick promised, undressing. He was naked within seconds, his hard flesh showing off powerful muscles as his hands reached for his belt.

Lisa's face was flushed, her eyes widening at the sight of what he was doing. Her mouth watered to taste his hard cock, which was now in full view. As his hand gripped the belt, the fingers from his other hand gripped the head of his hard cock, tugging at it teasingly as it pulsed and darkened with intense arousal. A tiny bead of pre-cum formed at the tip, glistening.

She had never been so aroused just by watching a man work his cock. She licked her lips in hunger while staring at the heavily veined flesh. Nick smiled when he saw how distracted she was. Just what he had wanted. She had also stopped struggling in the restraints, almost welcoming them.

Before she could do more than gasp in surprise, he undid her restraints and turned her around and ordered her to be still. The restraints were back on, but now her back was to him with her ass on full display. Lisa wasn't into the whole submission thing, spanking and toys, but she had no choice right now. She could be sincere and stop this, but she'd never been so turned on in her life and that included when Nick made her cum before.

He came up behind her, arms over her head and still like she was ordered and pressed his cock against her ass. His hands reached around her with one taking a hold of her left breast and the other going between her legs. He had put lube on his hands as if she wasn't wet enough.

Slowly, he slid his lubricated fingers inside her, one after the other, stretching her while she burned in desire. The forceful dominance was more arousing than she could have ever imagined, and the pain was desirable because she couldn't stop it.

"Just remain still," he ordered. He kept her still, stretching her pussy as he wanted while squeezing her nipples. His cock, still pressed firmly against her ass was emitting pre-cum and lubing her up in the forbidden hole she has never had touched.

Lisa just stood there on full display as his fingers fucked her while he aggressively played with her nipples. It was then that his hands were removed from her body and placed on her hips. His hand lowered to his cock, and he began to guide it. He reached up and loosened the restraints to lengthen them, allowing her a little freedom but just enough to have her slightly stick her ass out, which she did without order.

As it got close to her opened pussy, his free hand grabbed a hold of her neck and pulled her close to his face, slightly distorting her position. "Do you understand who I am yet?" he asked. But there weren't any words she could say to respond as she barely had enough air to breath, only nodding yes. She was in a zone and didn't want it to end.

Nick was in his own zone, unable to control his build to an orgasm as he pointed his rock hard cock toward her visibly open and wet entrance. The only thing stopping him from cumming was the delay in entering her. He needed inside her, but more than that he needed her to know that he had control over her, which also implied control over himself.

As he finally felt able enough to hold it, he slowly entered her, making her back arch, both from the sheer pleasure and the hand still around her neck. She couldn't move anything but her mouth, which was enough as her soft whimpers turned into uncontrollable moans in between panting.
The pain of his huge dick made her whimper in between moans but she'd never ask him to stop, no matter how hard it hurt.

"Ask me to do it harder, Lisa," Nick said, all too calmly like he didn't feel anything.

Lisa tried to look back but his grip on her neck prevented all but any small movement from her lips. "More please," she cried. She could barely breathe from her gasping.

Nick stopped and gripped tighter on her neck, positioning himself to prove a point. "What did I tell you to say, Lisa?" he said with a stern tone. She knew she had no choice, but her head was so foggy she could barely recall.

"Please fuck me harder," she said, hoping she had remembered correctly.

Nick's grip loosened and he entered her deeper than before. She was relieved that she had said it correctly and his choke didn't tighten more, but she also kept thinking what if she hadn't. Nick was now behind her giving her every inch when he stopped just shy of giving her his cum inside her aching pussy. "Please keep going," she begged in a whimpering type of tone.

"You need to know what I'm capable of first. You will get my cum, but it will be inside your swollen pussy."

"Swollen?" she responded with uncertainty of what he meant. It was already swollen from the building sexual tension. What the fuck else did he want?

Nick grabbed his belt and turned her from him, her ass on full display. Lisa immediately went in full defiant mode, "What the fuck are you doing, why aren't you fucking me?"

"I told you that I have the control here, and you need to know it." Nick said with a steady voice she wasn't comfortable with.

At that moment, his arm struck the belt against her ass which made nice loud pop. A movement of her body trying to escape was evident at first but eventually calmed down after a few seconds. A second swat of the belt popped her even better.

"Owww," was all she could whimper.

A third swat that really stung hit her ass. "What the fuck?" she whimpered as her ass began forming welts. She slightly tugged on her restraints, knowing she couldn't get away but trying to anyway.

All she could wonder was why he wanted to stop fucking her to do this and how she could stop this. A fourth swat made her basically buckle to the pain but immediately prop back up to prepare for a fifth. "Please fuck me," she whimpered in a desperate attempt to get him to stop but still get his cock.

"Please fuck me what?" he said, gripping the belt in a different way in order to achieve a bigger pop when it hit.

"Fuck me Master, fuck me Sir, fuck me Daddy, fuck me please," she kept going, wondering what he wanted to hear at the time.

Finally, she could hear the belt go down and he came up behind her. He undid her restraints and allowed her to relax. She immediately looked at him, confused about what he was doing. Certainly, he wasn't stopping again?

This was the time Nick wanted to test her. To see her obedience. He controlled her physically, but did he have her mind? That was the test.

"Come over here little girl and bend over," Nick said as he gripped his still rigid cock.

Lisa did as she was told. She may not have been restrained but she was no longer the brat. If only for tonight, she has fully submitted to him. Nick rubbed his cock up and down her pussy and ass. She had never had anal sex before, but she didn't move when it touched her forbidden entrance. She was his, and he knew it after that.

But Nick wasn't ready to take that from her, he wanted her pussy she barely kept from dripping down her legs. As Nick entered her, she let out a moan of relief, finally getting what she has needed for so long, especially tonight. Nick thrusted and thrusted, his strong arms holding her hips as he pounded into her now loose pussy.

"Oh, fuck," she said with all the energy she had as he slammed into her. It was then that he let out a few loud gasps and moans, and she felt his cum shooting inside her. Lisa was in ecstasy even more than Nick was. Lisa had not cum but she didn't care. She was humiliated but turned on more than ever in her life. She got fucked by the man who controlled more than he thinks he does.

"Are you okay, little girl?" Nick asked as he let her loose from any verbal or physical restraints.

"Yes, sir," was immediately released from her lips as she laid on the bed.

After this, Nick held Lisa as she came down from the moment she had just experienced. Last time, Nick was a complete asshole but this time he wasn't. Lisa finally began to understand that the way to Nick was being an obedient good girl.

Chapter Ten.

The office was relatively calm. To the right, tinkering could be heard from the slightly open kitchen door. To the left, Allen's door was wide open. His office was a cluster of disorganized papers that annoyed him. But he couldn't help it. Allen was calm and orderly, but this case has rattled him. That and his growing affection towards Lisa that he kept hidden.

His camera lay on the side of his table where he had kept it after emptying its memory into his laptop. He had wheeled the transparent board into the office and had added more papers to it. They knew more now and had to group the facts.

Alex had shot Phoebe. Then he shot himself while the psychotic Jamal watched. But it didn't explain who killed the other three people: Sylvester Donovan, Jeanne Evans, and Christie Harrison. All fingers still point to Jamal. The second group had been easy to link together–they all had the same batch of cocaine flowing through their system. But cocaine didn't give bullet and stab wounds. *A fight over cocaine might...* It sounded so believable in his head. If only he could prove it. The last murders happened in the parking lot of a fancy restaurant a little way off Praxton, and it was the most confusing of them all. *Engagement party gone wrong.* They all didn't add up, leaving a loose thread that mocked him. He hated it.

He paced the room–to get blood flowing to his brain as he had told Lisa–stopping only at the board and his desk to go through files and papers again. He looked like a deranged man. With his hair left in loose waves, brushing his shoulders and framing his spectacled face and his cuffed, wrinkled shirt. His eyes were burned from behind his glasses, angry yet droopy.

He needed a break. More than that he needed to sleep. But it was Thursday already, and Halloween was a day away. He valued his reputation more than his sleep. He broke his back-and-forth pacing, deciding on a cup of coffee. He could hear Lisa doing whatever she liked doing in there. It had become a place where delicious smells rose from, and a pot of coffee was always ready. Her magic didn't end there. The office was tidier, as she gave her best effort to keep his papers in order. He suspected she cleaned up Nick's apartment too–when they weren't around.

She was a good choice; one he had needed. He remembered the day they had a moment to talk about life and her ambitions. Young and inexperienced about life, but she was passionate and determined. She was very pretty, but her beauty was more than that. Her smile could light up the room, but it was her intelligence and ability to hold a conversation that really got to him. But as smart as she was, he always felt like she needed guidance and nurturing as she navigated her days.

He felt a passion for her when she was near, but he knew she was half his age. He felt a fierce need to protect her, even from himself. He knew their age gap would be an issue for a real relationship, and although he liked her, he knew it would be forbidden with someone that worked for him. So, this is how it would stay: him holding his feelings back and remaining a father figure… a daddy figure. That made him smile.

He listened to her light footsteps again; a smile playing on his lips. *Yes, I can hold back anything to see you safe and happy.* He stood by his office door, watching her until his drowsiness dulled his thoughts.

"Lisa?" he called, dropping to the nearest couch. The noise from the kitchen stopped.
 "Can I have some coffee?"

"Yes sir Mr. Bolton," came the reply. It was soft enough to set goosebumps on his skin. He let out an audible moan accompanied by a smile as he slacked on the couch. He knew now was not the time to dwell on desire, but he was drowning in it.

He zoned in the tick-tock of the clock, taking deep breaths and fighting to keep his eyes open. They drooped with a mind of their own and yawns escaped his lips. He raised a hand to his eye and paused when he met no obstacle. *Right. I forgot.* He had taken off his glasses in frustration.

The kitchen door creaked open, and Lisa appeared with a white tray. She shrugged and offered him a sweet smile that he needed to see.

"What took you so long?" he asked sarcastically with an obviously playful grin.

She lightly set the tray on the table, giving a short and equally sarcastic eye roll. The tray had a single steaming mug of swirling coffee, a teaspoon and a small container with cream. "I wanted it to be perfect, just for you, and perfection takes time – and on your part, patience." Her voice was lighter than he remembered–softer too–and her tone was sultry.

Allen had already been daydreaming about her and didn't want this moment to end. "Well, perfect would have meant you put the cream in for me, wouldn't it?" he asked with his own eye roll, mocking her in a way that was more flirty than sarcastic.

She kneeled, causing the tight skirt she wore to ride up her thighs. "Tell me when to stop?" she asked, picking up the container. She tilted it, letting cream pour into the cup, turning the dark liquid lighter.

"Perfect," he said as she got the poured an adequate amount in the cup. Little did she know that he wasn't even looking at the cup but was looking at her. From the top of her head to the few inches of cleavage her top allowed him to see.

When she looked back at him, she could tell Allen was staring at her all along and paid no attention to the coffee. She forgot the words she was about to say or even what universe she was in as she was lost in the moment. For a moment that seemed like an eternity, they both stood still, eyes locked, neither flinching.

"Is… there…. anything else you… need?" Lisa asked with a slight biting of her lower lip, not knowing what answer she would get but knowing what answer she wanted. She knew he would be disappointed to know what she had done with Nick, but right now Nick wasn't there and she hadn't had a moment like this in a very long time - if she ever even had one.

Allen responded in a way that she couldn't understand. "Why don't I ask if there is something you need?" Allen asked, sitting up straighter, eyes fixated on her.

There was a calmness in his eyes, different that Nick's, but similar. A boldness that he had control of the situation but welcoming enough to have her eyes start to tear up as she unwillingly began to let go of her boxed in emotions. *How is he doing this?*

"Come here," he asked in a calm voice and took out his hand. Something in his voice was soothing, yet the words came out dominant. She couldn't stop herself even if she tried. She grabbed his hand as he sat her on the couch. "You don't have to tell me what is wrong, but you have every opportunity to. I can tell you wear a mask every day you come to work."

He brought Lisa over on his lap. She was lying sideways where he couldn't see but the side of her face. Her body went limp as his soothing voice whispered, "Just lie there and relax." It brought a calmness to her as if she had just received a massage. She just let go in the moment, doing as she was told. She didn't realize that her hair had fallen and covered her face until Allen ran his hands over her it and tucked it behind her head.

Allen heard a faint sniffle, and he repeated, "Just relax, Lisa, you're safe." Allen was on fire with this.

He had always thought about taking care of someone much younger, but it wasn't until Lisa was there, in this moment, that he felt a little high, like he was meant for this. *She thinks I'm taking care of her, but she is taking care of me.*

At any moment, Lisa felt like he was going to start rubbing her breasts or ass, but it never came. Just her lying there while he just played with her hair and stroked her face was turning her on. Maybe it was her experience with Nick and every other asshole guy she had ever known, but almost instinctively she positioned her body to allow his hands to roam where they wanted.

Allen looked down over her body and although his eyes roamed, his hands didn't. He wanted her to feel safe, and that meant from his desires as well. He wanted to fuck her as bad as he's ever wanted to fuck any woman in his life, but not right now. Right now, he wanted to be whatever she needed him to be, and that was her protector.

"You ok, little one?" he asked, breaking the silence as her sniffles subsided.

Smiling ear to ear at those words, "Why did you call me that?" she asked.

"Just came natural, I guess," he responded, not really knowing the answer himself, "Maybe it is because although you are an adult, you are so much younger than me, so it just came out?" His response almost sounded like a question, but not necessarily to her.

Lisa was lost in silence, her head clear of everything: her bills piling up, her desire for Nick, her crazy ex-boyfriend. Just plain clear. Allen had put her in a trance she had never been in. For the first time in forever, she felt safe and taken care of.

"Sit up, I need to get back to the case," Allen said, trying to clear his head from the situation.

Lisa sat up, but didn't move, as she was only instructed to rise. Her trance had her in a submissive zone, but not sexually. Like a child that had followed their parents' guidance because they hadn't yet learned the world, Lisa awaited further instruction. Allen reached out and hugged her as she hugged him back. Cheek to cheek, they embraced in a tight hug, each slightly rubbing the other's back. As their faces both leaned back, their hands kept their grip on the other's back, not allowing more than an inch or so of gap between their lips.

"Do you feel better?" Allen asked.

Lisa didn't even know she had felt bad. Yet Allen had almost instantly made her break down and relieve herself of so much anxiety and tension with his words and gentle touch. "Yes, thank you," Lisa replied. Her eyes basically begged him to kiss her.

They both loosened their grip on each other and backed away. Lisa stood up, and Allen stood behind her as if to walk her out as both glanced at the clock, realizing the time.

"Why don't you go get some rest, I need to down your perfect coffee and see if it is the magic to help me with this case," Allen said.

"Okay, sounds good," Lisa said, slightly coming out of her trance.

"Okay, sounds good? That is your response after that moment we had?" Allen said with a smile and small chuckle. Allen knew he was still in control of the situation; he just wanted her to acknowledge it. He needed her to acknowledge that he just took care of her.

"Umm, yes, sir?" she said very light with a smile and squinting eyes, as if she were looking for his approval.

"Sir will be fine for tonight," Allen responded, as if he wanted her to be proud of herself for getting it right, "but don't say it like I'm your boss. Say it like you enjoyed our cuddling on the couch. You can always come to me if something is wrong. You may not know this, but I enjoyed you lying there as much as you did."

Lisa could just feel the honesty coming from Allen. She turned away, flushed but happy. Lightheaded but a little more aware now that her trance was coming down. Her mind stayed on Allen the entire night. She felt like a high schooler with a crush who finally asked her out. As Lisa lay there in her bed, she thought about using her dildo as she normally did before she went to sleep. But as she pulled off her underwear and pulled out her favorite vibrator, she had no desire for it despite how turned on she was.

Instead, Lisa put her underwear back on, turned off the lights, and laid back down. Her mind was on that moment shared with Allen as it had been from the moment she had said goodbye. As she got lost in her daydream, Lisa's hands lightly rolled over her night t-shirt, grazing her nipples. In her mind it was Allen lightly touching her. They went down, resting on her stomach, playing with the waist band of her underwear. In her daydream, Allen was teasing her, and her hands were doing exactly what she thought his hands would be doing.

Slowly working her own fingers under her waistband, Lisa pulled them out and lightly rubbed her lips outside her panties instead of under. She immediately felt like a virgin being touched for the first time as a jolt of calming energy went through her body. Her eyes rolled in the back of her head as her fingers parted her lips and pushed her panties slightly inside. *Oh my god.* Feeling like she was touched for the first time, she only used her index finger and pressed the fabric against her clit.

Her mind visualizing Nick rubbing her while she lay on his lap. She orgasmed within seconds of rubbing her clit. Her body convulsed while her finger never quickened or slowed the pace of pushing her fabric against her clit. She needed it to be Allen's gentle touch, and she did everything she could to mimic her thoughts.

Panting and completely out of energy, she finally came to her senses as her orgasm subsided. Normally her fantasies would go away after she came. But this was different. In her mind, he was still there, about to hold her to sleep, and she kept the fantasy going. She took her panties off as they were soaking wet but had no energy to get a fresh pair. She just lay there on her side, being in a "little spoon" position with Allen behind her. After a few moments of feeling safe, she drifted off to sleep.

***

Nick never understood people's obsession with money. They could go all out to get it and conceive any possible plan to achieve immediate payback for the least amount of work. It was sickening–a rot that had eaten its way into the heart of the young. He wouldn't call himself rich but with his job and veteran perks, he lived comfortably. But many people don't, and he knew that.

If there was one thing he had learned from talking with all the *newly rich* in Praxton, it was that people are either greedy and vain or desperate and ruthless. Who could he blame? Those who committed crimes to be rich? Or those who are living large off the backs of their dead relatives?

How many rich people do we have in Praxton? Something was fishy, he knew. He had gone the extra mile to report his suspicion to the station and asked for the records of some suspects. If he dug deep enough into their history and lives, he would figure it out before the police if there was something there.

He had been so agitated by the case that he was out of it until he heard the sound of laughter. He chuckled. *When did I get here?* He was watching children play - two boys. The blonde one looked older than the boy with sandy brown hair. They kicked a small blue ball between each other close to the curb. Other children played on the swings and merry-go-round.

He paused, tucking his hands in his pocket. The memories of playing baseball with Allen in his backyard while his mother made sweet tea and brownies for them bloomed in his mind. A lot of his afternoons went that way. They returned from school together, and sometimes Allen ate dinner at his house and others times he ate at Allen's. It had been years, but just as he and Allen were inseparable as friends growing up, they never lost touch or slowed communication as they moved along their career paths. They always encouraged each other as they progressed through the ranks of their professions, but there was also a sense of competition and who had the bigger career dick. It made them both better and it made them both successful.

Nick knew Allen's past, and it made him get lost in the moment of how they had gotten here. Neither man had been able to settle down and have children or get married. Nick had a few relationships, nothing more than a year and nothing past fake "I love you's" and what seemed like fuck buddy roommates rather than girlfriends. Nick was bored easily with women and knew he would never be able to sustain any form of commitment, so he didn't even try. Nick knew Allen had tried to settle a few times but seemed to always get fucked over by women. Either he was too nice, spent too much time at work or he was too "fill in the blank".

He was hardened by all his relationship failures and seemed to be turning into Nick every passing day with a "fuck it" attitude. And Nick, idolizing his best friend, tried to become more and more like Allen and find that compassion, but he just couldn't. But in the end, they both were who they were to the core, and they were a better team for it. Both knew what the other was thinking and complimented each other's styles like twin brothers. *No, better than twin brothers*. Each would take a bullet for the other without hesitation.

Back to reality, Nick watched the sandy brown boy kick the ball high in the air. It soared and rolled off the curb into the road. The boy ran for it while the other screamed for him and pursued him. Nick sighed at their carelessness and walked closer. The boy went to the ball and picked it up. The blonde boy then reached for him, grabbing his hand, starting what looked to be a small rant. This distracted them as they were paying attention to each other and not the road. *Wrong move.*

Nick saw the flash of red coming ahead, accompanied by loud music. The boys were too engrossed in their argument to notice, and he moved on instinct. He placed his hands around his mouth and screamed, "Hey!" The boys stopped arguing and turned to stare at him. They didn't turn to look at the car. *Shit!* He shook his head. The car would collide with them any second.

With a sharp right, he ran into the road, waving his hands at the car instead. It didn't stop. *Who the hell is driving that thing?!* He increased his pace and stood right behind the boys who were frozen in place at the oncoming car. They clung to his legs immediately making it harder for him to move himself or them. *Shit!* He groaned, scooting closer to the curb.

He jumped out of the way, seconds before the car drove past them, the driver bringing his hand through the window, giving him the finger. *Yeah well, fuck you too for not slowing down.* Nick ignored the driver and looked down to give the boys a scolding of their life only to find the sandy blonde in tears, still clutching to his legs. *Oh, no.* He saw the boy clean snot on his trousers. *Screw this. It was just children being careless as usual. Where in the heck are their parents?*

"You alright there little buddy?" he said in his softest voice. The blonde nodded but the brunette still bawled. "Where are your parents?" he tried again.

"She's… she's at work, mister, and I don't have a dad," the blonde answered.

She left two children unsupervised for work! She's the one who needs talking to.

"Where does she work?" he asked before realizing they might not know.

"At the detective's office two blocks away."

Oh! Nick smiled. *Now, this is a surprise.* "You know the way there?" The blonde nodded. "Let's get you, boys, to your mom."

That was how he found himself led by small hands to his own office. He felt particularly giddy when the building came into view. He held the door open for them and waited for the action to happen. They walked in on cautious feet and not a moment later Lisa appeared, alerted by the doorbell.

She stopped in her tracks with a gasp at the sight of the little boy. "Mommy!" they screamed, rushing towards her. Her eyes moved from them, and Nick caught her embarrassed gaze. *What an interesting woman you are, Lisa Monroe.* He smirked just before she looked away. In a moment, Nick learned more about Lisa than all the previous moments combined and suddenly a form of empathy filled his mind. She wasn't just a cocky, hot secretary trying to get her own career going. She was a single mother struggling to get by. That was the secret he longed to know.

Chapter Eleven.

"Why did you keep it from me? From us?" he half smirked in disappointment. "Where's their father? Nick asked.

It was Lisa's idea to go out to lunch with Nick to talk things out. Allen had offered to keep an eye on the boys as he downloaded and deciphered some additional information from the station database.

Lisa had developed feelings both for Nick and for Allen, completely different but they were deep. The moments with Nick were exactly what she needed to open her up sexually to a level she had never been, and the moment with Allen was exactly what she needed to open her up romantically. But each had also taken her past where she was. Every time she was around Nick, she immediately got wet and every time she was around Allen, she immediately calmed down and felt safe. But in this moment, Nick was kind and gentle and made her feel like she could be open.

"We're divorced, and he is no longer around," she began. "Met him in college. I was funding my college tuition when we started dating. I left my broken home at an early age since my family had been torn apart after my father's passed. My mother became an alcoholic and could no longer care for me, so I left. I met Matt, the father, at one of the stores where I had worked part-time, and we kind of hit it off. He took advantage of my naiveness, and we eloped once I found out I was pregnant.

"Matt was quite comfortable financially, he had a supportive family, though he hardly mentioned them or visited. Before Matt, I never liked anyone other than a few high school flings. Anyway, Matt was fun and took care of me," Lisa chuckled, trying to lighten the heavy atmosphere, but Nick didn't laugh. His eyes were blank, but his clenched fists let her know that he wasn't going to take whatever she had to say lightly.

"Matt became my family. I moved in with him. Since we didn't have a wedding, it didn't really seem like a real marriage, just us living together as good friends. Anyway, he wasn't ready for a baby, and neither was I. But we had Matthew, named after him and tried to make it a go as a family. And it worked for a while, he made the money, and I basically quit everything to be a mom and wife. And not long after he was born, I found out that I was pregnant again. So, we continued acting like a family, except I wasn't acting. I was falling in love with being a wife and mother."

"Where did it go wrong? That's what I want to know," Nick cut in. "He is no longer here for his boys. Even if you and he didn't work, that's fucked up. I'm not a father but I had one, and he was a good dad even when he left my mom."

"Well, he started cheating, became abusive, came home less. He wasn't the Matt I knew. I started slowly slipping into depression as he started slipping… well… into other women." Lisa's eyes started to water; Nick could tell she was fighting emotion. "It got worse as the days went by. It's like he cared less and less about the boys and me the more women he had. One day, the boys and I went out, but the weather shorted our plans. I caught him with a young girl on our couch. I had walked in with my sons right behind me. It was devastating to see even though they were too young to really know what was going on. So, we moved in with my mom, and I never looked back."

Nick smiled. He had texted the name Matthew McClain to Allen and knew Allen was already on it. Background check, current employment, etc. All he needed to text was a name and he knew. *Better than twin brothers.*

Lisa continued, unaware of what Allen and Nick were doing by text. "Apparently, he had always had a thing for younger women," Lisa continued. "Not just any young woman. Those who looked petite, frail, fragile, and alone. It seemed like he fed off their misery and vulnerability. He'd support them and give them a sense of purpose, and in return, they, without even realizing it, made him a god in their lives. I did too."

"It was different with me because I worked hard, too. It was an even effort. Don't get me wrong, I had made my husband my god too. I worshipped him because I felt like he took care of us. And he did financially, but that's where it ended." The tears couldn't be held back despite using the dinner napkin from the restaurant.

"When things started to fall apart, I started falling apart too. I saw the signs and ignored them, trying to keep things normal for my boys." Lisa tensed up, attempting to look tough as she regained full awareness of her surroundings.

"Some guys just can't handle responsibility," Nick said, being overly blunt. "For a long time, I probably would have done the same thing. I never settled because I know I can leave a woman, but I sure as hell know I could never leave my kids. So, I didn't have any."

It was the first time Lisa had heard any sort of commitment from Nick. Not for a woman, but for children. The man whose last name could have easily been his nickname finally showed a soft spot - for children. And not just any children. Children of his own. And even though he didn't, Lisa could see he meant every word. If Nick was anything, he was blunt and honest.

"So, here I am," Lisa continued. "I need money and waitressing just isn't cutting it. I don't trust men, so I won't try and find one, and I have honestly always had a passion for criminal journalism. So, when I saw this case on the news not far from where I lived, I checked it out. Then I saw the ad for a secretary, did a little research on you guys, and took a leap. Make money while learning how detectives solve cases. I never knew that…"

Nick cut her off, "I think I've heard enough."

There is the asshole again. "What do you mean?" Lisa stumbling through her words as he cut her off spilling her life to him.

"We have a case to solve, and you have boys to take care of."

Nick was acting like an asshole father, but he was right. They didn't have time to spend all day going back and forth about shattered hopes and dreams if they were to solve the case. Lisa told him the story and she told him the truth. For the first time since the early days of Matt, she let herself become open and honest.

"I'm not a trainwreck, you know, " Lisa asserted. She spoke to Nick but was really talking to herself. "I have my shit together," she chuckled, basically begging for a reply.

"If I thought you were a trainwreck, we wouldn't be here. If I thought you were a shitty mom, we wouldn't be here. If you think I came to listen to your story because of your sweet ass looks and wanting to fuck you again, think again. I can fuck almost any heartbroken woman in the city and trust me, in Las Vegas, I can barely pull my dick out without touching one," Nick said, again being honest in a way that only he could. "It is your personality and charm that really gets to me. I've never been able to sit and talk to a woman and not become bored."

Was that Nick's way of flirting? How is he such an asshole but such a turn-on at the same time? "Shall we go see what Allen has?" she followed up.

"Yes, we need to see what he has come up with. Time is getting pretty short. My patience is getting shorter."

A buzz hit Nick's phone as he barely slipped it out of his pocket to read the screen. It was a text from Allen. "Loser is in prison for thinking he was meeting a seventeen-year-old, but actually met an undercover cop. He's isolated now but won't make it out alive."

A sense of disgust rolled over Nick's mind, followed by a short sense of relief. *Looks like I don't have to deal with the fucker myself.* He knew he wanted to protect Lisa. He didn't know what from, but beating the shit out of Matt would serve multiple purposes right now. Now that Nick felt that Lisa was forever protected from him, he needed the stress relief. He was timing it perfectly as his eyes went down to Lisa's perfectly shaped ass, begging to be released from her skirt. Finally, a smile.

Lisa could feel his eyes on her ass as she walked toward her car, parallel parked on the street a few blocks from the restaurant. She knew he wanted her and knew she wanted it. *Fuck, just the other day I could only have Allen in my thoughts and right now all I want is Nick to bend me over these cars and put me on full display.* "What the fuck is wrong with me?" she said silently to herself.

"I can tell you are putting it on display right now," Nick said, back in asshole mode. "But the only thing you'd be getting today was a spanking. I'm not fucking people that work for me whenever they want. I fuck on *my* time."

"You're such an asshole," Lisa said as she unlocked the car with her fob. Here I am pouring my heart out to you, and you talk to me like that."

"Don't call your boss an asshole. You poured your heart out back at the table. When we started walking, you poured that sweet little ass in the air to flaunt it."

This time Nick chuckled as if to bring out more bratty talk from Lisa. Nick was very into her being confident and defiant as it was way sexier to break a wild stallion than to ride a broken pony.

Lisa's pussy was wet, and she hated it. She hated that his blunt honesty and confidence drove her so crazy. And the fierce protective words while being empathetic at the table only boosted her feelings for him, as up to this point they had only been sexual. She was falling in love with Nick Stone, and she knew it.

***

Back in the office, Allen had been working, trying to piece all that had happened together as Nick and Lisa walked in.

"These people are blowing our phones up," Allen said.

"What do you expect? Halloween is on Saturday. They're trying to play it safe. Attend every call with an assertive assurance, Lisa," Nick ordered. "You'd think they'd be calling because of the robberies," He dropped onto the nearest couch.

"People are hedonistic and superficial. Halloween is way more important than a few robberies… and multiple murder cases," Allen scoffed, drumming on the table with his fingers. He had dragged over the board that held the photos and all his paper cutouts, clipping, and news linking all the cases; the robberies took a lesser space than the three groups of murder.

"Halloween would have helped though," Lisa sighed, moving closer to the board. "It was a perfect opportunity to observe the scene. A night where suspects would less cautious."

"Maybe a few of those newly rich would be rendered intoxicated at a bar," Nick said, massaging his temples. "Or one of the corpses would suddenly resurrect." He chuckled while Lisa seethed. She was throwing the first thing she could lay her hands on: an empty pack of push pins. It soared in the air but fell at his feet.

Nick stared at the pack and laughed at her attempt. "No offense, but Halloween won't change things. I've scoured Praxton. Same tale everywhere. Our newly rich is said to have inherited wealth from some distant relative–which is true. I looked it up. They are in no way related to the recent robberies."

"I thought we dropped that case," Allen yawned, taking his glasses off.

"We did. Or rather the station did." He sucked on his cheek from inside his mouth. "Sarg verified the family relations alibi, and it's not related to the robberies in any way."

"And we are going to buy that?" Allen arched his brow.

"If we want," smirked Nick. "There are too many possible links to the murders for me to let it go that easily."

"What about your report?" Allen yawned again before turning to the board. He stretched his back and raised a hand to strip the board of the photos.

"Turned it in, as a case solved." Nick crossed his chest and watched Lisa. Her eyes were trained on Allen. "Sarg could care less. He ranted about the homicide after receiving a few calls from the mayor."

"I see…" Allen mumbled, still fixated on the board. "The pressure is on us now," He chuckled, and some unhung photos slipped from his hand. He turned to stare at them.

Lisa stood up straight and hurried to pick them up, right about the same time Allen bent to pick them up. They collided, bumping heads, and all the photos in Allen's hand scattered, littering the floor.

Nick chuckled, rising to his feet. "The pressure is real, you guys okay?"

Lisa turned crimson at his comment and dropped to grab the photos. Allen crouched low to help her. Nick stopped in his tract and leaned on the wall instead.

"It's fine, it's fine," she protested. "It's my fault. Let me…"

"It's nobody's fault, Lisa," Allen laughed, giving her that look that always calmed her." The pressure is mounting, that's all." Lisa ignored him, trying with frantic hands to gather them all up. "Calm down,"

Allen advised in a stern tone. It wasn't like Nick's tone, but it was still enough to get her to firm up.

"Truly, Lisa, you don't have to put yourself under pressure." Nick tried to calm her. She looked at him only for an instant and turned to the photos.

Instead of picking them up, she began turning them over. Allen followed her lead. They paused, stared at each other, and continued.

"Would you look at that?" Allen cried in laughter and Lisa smiled like she just won the jackpot.

"What?" Nick asked, eager to know, but he held his place by the wall.

"Our biggest clue yet," Allen smiled, standing to his feet and Lisa followed suit.

Chapter Twelve.

This has the characteristics of what Nick termed a "fuck me" moment. Everyone felt stupid for not seeing it earlier. He felt incredibly stupid for not paying more attention, especially when something that obvious was staring right at him. This had only happened once before that Nick could remember. The culprit had been right there all along–an older cousin– but he was rather beloved by the dead victim and had a clean slate everywhere. They couldn't pin it on him until they found the victim's diary hidden amongst her overflowing personal library courtesy of the victim. He had felt more foolish because he liked the boy too.

At least he had a second one to add to his portfolio. The word "Boo" was the furthest thing on his mind when Lisa started her obsessive rearranging with Allen. Now it was imprinted on his memory.

"Maybe Boo is just another clue," Lisa broke the silence, shifting back with crossed arms.

"Instead of overthinking It, let's just go with the obvious: it just means boo. A word that should spread fear." Allen chuckled, taking off his glasses. "A practical joke of some sort."

"A bloody joke?" Lisa scoffed.

"No," answered Nick. Leaning on the wall, his eyes fell on the board again. "A coincidental one, perpetrated by the one person who had nothing to lose and was confident in each murder scene."

It was impossible that all three scenes were connected except by one person.

"There were no survivors," Lisa quipped. "Who would have known about all three–"

"Nicklaus!" Allen slammed his hand on the table, causing Lisa to jump. Nick smiled when their eyes met.

"But…" Lisa's mouth gaped like a fish, and she turned shocked eyes to Nick. "Mr. Stone couldn't… he… it can't be,"

"I have no flair for theatrics," he chuckled. "But I know a Niklaus who does, and so do you." Nick watched the gears turn in Lisa's head, changing her open lips into an "oh". He nodded and ran a hand through his hair. "It makes a lot of sense now; Niklaus Peters was the common thread."

Nick hated interrogating the family and friends of the victims, but he picked up a lot. Whenever women were allowed to talk freely, they would always derail. Once they did, it was time to take note. It was during such sessions he heard Niklaus's name mentioned first.

"The group killed at the parking lot of The Solar quarter past eleven was Niklaus' first appearance that night." He said pointing at the five bodies shaped like a "B".

"Family affair turned mass murder. Turns out his brother Mr. Eli Peters suffered from a case of schizophrenia. He has undergoing treatment for years of course but snapped while drunk. Putting a bullet–"

"Who the hell gave a madman a gun?!" snapped Lisa. He choked on laughter at her comment, causing her face to go red.

"Good question." He cleared his throat and continued, "Who do you think?" He didn't need her reply before continuing his story. "The giver in question happened to be settling the bill inside after the proprietor pleaded with the drunk group to leave. He was held up for a moment on a call when rapid fire was heard. Guess who called?"

"Phoebe Gerald," chuckled Allen. "To tell him she was with his child. Only she never got the chance to tell him and that's why he was surprised when I told him."

Lisa wrinkled her forehead in thought, looking from Nick to Allen. "How is this all fitting now? Where has all this information been hiding?!"

"In our heads," Nick said, pushing himself off the wall. "Follow carefully, little Lisa, or you might get lost in the woods." He smirked when she shot daggers at him with her gaze.

"She did send him her location and an SOS when Alex started his performance. Quite a jealous lover,"

"Petty too. He couldn't even share…" Allen shook his head suggesting displeasure, only to chuckle the next second. Nick laughed too, but at Lisa's expense. Her confused look amused him.

"Where were we? Ah, yes! Niklaus hung up on her and ran back to his group to find them bleeding out. As their designated driver and the one not intoxicated, he pushed all five of them–strong man– into his truck that somehow caught on fire a day before he left."

"He received Phoebe's SOS on the way to the hospital." Allen walked up to him.

"And made a detour, for love," said Nick, locking eyes with Allen.

"Group two. Four friends were having a small dinner when Alex showed up angry and a lover's quarrel ensued. In anger at her promiscuity, he shot her. Chaos followed and he had the balls to silence everyone there with his gun."

"But couldn't stand to pay for his crimes. He silenced himself. The perfect crime," mused Nick.

"For love," sighed Lisa, something she couldn't fathom happening to her again but every you girl's daydream.

"And pride… and bitterness." Allen pursed his lips. "Imagine Niklaus's mental state when he arrived at his amor's house."

"It got more fucked up, that's for sure." Nick tried not to laugh; it was not the time for it.

He looked at Lisa's reaction, wanting to tease her, but instead met a sad face. "He must have been so confused." Her voice echoed with pity, "So much blood and loss, in one night? It's enough to turn any sane man mad."

"Agreed. Stacie observed pressure was applied on Phoebe's wound."

"He tried to save her," Lisa whispered, pressing one hand to her mouth and the other flat on her chest. Nick saw the silvery trail of tears leak from her eyes first. *It isn't worth the tears, darling.* He froze in place watching them fall before Allen turned. He was beside her in a heartbeat and wrapped her in a hug.

"It was all he could do before realizing she was gone," he heard Allen whisper. Watching Allen hold Lisa while she cried gave him a comforting smile, making him glad he didn't have to do it. Allen was way better suited for that type of coddling.

"The last group was pure coincidence. Sergeant Rick would give the details better, but I know they've been following a drug case and well, they just got their biggest witness–Niklaus."

Nick had to pause for this one. He had been churning the details in his mind for quite some time. "Niklaus so happened to live opposite some druggies who had recently changed dealers. They had set up a small business supplying to their clique and of course, their neighbor, Niklaus."

"I had heard about that," Lisa muttered and frowned when Nick gave her a surprised look. "What? I live in Praxton too… I hear things."

"Oh-kay, I'll take that and say you have the makings of a good detective." He saw her frown change to a smile before continuing. "It was good stuff or so I heard, and people started stealing for it. That is what is causing the increase in crime. Some of them escaped when the previous kings of Praxton's drug scene busted their joint, and their product is still in circulation."

"Hence the constant robberies…" Allen stared out the window. "This changes Praxton's playing field."

"Exactly," Nick agreed. "But none of this concerned Niklaus. He had needed help disposing of the bodies,"

"Or he needed a fix to forget his sorrow," Allen added.

"Or give him courage for what he was about to do," Lisa shivered.

Nick paused to watch his co-narrators. He waited until he was sure they had nothing to add and spoke. "He found the third stash of bodies. It flipped his switch. At first, we thought the bodies carried traces of alcohol because a lot of them had been drinking that night."

"But thanks to you," Allen turned to Lisa, giving her a pinch on her cheek, "the bottle of whisky and discarded lighter the officers found made sense–he wanted to burn them. Perhaps burn Praxton Avenue in the process."

"It had caused him too much pain and frustration, in one night," Lisa muttered.

"He chickened out though, after spelling out the word 'Boo' for whatever weird reason and dousing the bodies with the whiskey. He just left into the shadows and that's how we found them." He paused to let it sink in, the details clearing up as they brainstormed the situation.

The trio kept still, mulling over the potential full picture. One thing was for certain, Niklaus Peters was technically innocent of murder. He only made it difficult by putting the bodies in one place.

It was Lisa who asked the right question. "So… what do we do now?" Her eyes flicked from him to Allen.

He smirked and walked over to her. "We go buy ourselves some candy and prep our customers,"

Lisa's eyes lost the sadness and her lips lifted in a smile. "The boys would be delighted to hear that."

***

Nick emptied the second bag of mixed candy Lisa made into the bowl watching Allen wave their latest group of children goodnight. The office glowed orange and red–Lisa's swift decorating–casting dark shadows on the walls and making their amateur cobwebs and skulls look real. It wasn't scary on the inside but the ominous glow that fell on the curb from the slits in the aged black curtain they had covered the glass with worked. People flocked in. Many came to say, "thank you", and many more came for candy.

Allen's smile dropped the moment the door closed. He let out a tired groan and Nick laughed. "We should have left the case unsolved. At least until after Halloween."

"It was Halloween or our heads," Nick commented when he moved past him for the kitchen.

"Our heads would have made a fine monument, don't you think?" asked Allen from the kitchen.

"Maybe," Nick grabbed a Snicker bar from the bowl.

He was in the process of popping a piece into his mouth when Allen returned with a can of Mountain Dew at hand. "That's bad for you,"

"That's bad for you too." Nick eyed his drink.

"I'm not the one who–" The bell above the front door signaled someone had walked in. "Just a moment of peace is all we ask for," Allen groaned and moved for the reception.

He didn't make it across the room before Lisa appeared by the door with two little heads peeking from under her red billowing dress. The boys ran out the moment she waved them in. Allen bent to his knees and caught them in a hug and Nick picked up the bowl of candy.

"Trick or treat!" they chorused, giggling like they were already on a sugar rush. He ruffled their hair and came to stand beside Lisa.

"Nice of you to join us, Miss?" He eyed her red velvet dress and red cape. *Oh!*

"Red Riding Hood," She said and gave him a cheeky smile, "At your service."

"Red suits you," he praised, turning to watch Allen offer the boys some candy. "And where prey is, so is the wolf. Somebody needs to try to eat you,"

"No need," she smiled, watching the boys who she dressed like pirates thrill Allen with tales of their night. "My wolf lurks in this very room, waiting to devour me."

There is definitely a wolf in the room lurking.

***

Allen had made the decision that Nick and Lisa should take a few days off while he presented the conclusion to the station. Lisa had prepped the documents and Nick made them orderly, but it was Allen who was always in charge of presenting it to the guests at the station and arranging final payment.

"This was a hell of a case," Sergeant Rick said, shaking Allen's hand in approval. "There is no way we would have had the time for this. Regardless of the conclusion, it had to be over. The streets were becoming more and more dangerous at the thought a serial killer could be on the loose."

Allen walked out, smiling ear to ear that the case had been solved. He had texted Nick and Lisa and called for a celebration dinner. Nick was already waiting down in the office when Lisa arrived, two bottles of alcohol in her hand, lifting them in the air like a high schooler arriving at a house party.

"Cute," said Nick, where are the boys.

Lisa beamed ear to ear. "After we solved the case, I realized that when Matt was gone, I shouldn't have blacklisted his entire family. Although Matt's parents were never going to be great grandparents, Matt's grandmother was an amazing woman. So, I reached out and we spent a solid two hours catching up. She even filled me in on Matt's situation."

"Yeah, sorry about that," Nick cut in.

"Wait you knew you sorry motherfucker," Lisa responded in a very playful tone, trying to push Nick.

"I'm a detective, you don't think I can type a name into a computer?" Nick responded, his muscular body not moving at all by her push. "Rather, that Allen can?"

"He knows?" sighed Lisa.

"We are detectives." Nick concluded the argument.

"Anyway, she came down from Reno and has been spending the last few days with us. I remember now why she was the only one I liked in that family. She is amazing with the boys." Lisa beamed. "She said she would take them for the night when I told her I wanted to celebrate. You guys bought them pizza with the card by the way."

They had given Lisa a spare company credit card she hadn't needed to use until now, as Allen had texted her more than Nick and basically gave her permission, using the text "Do what you need to do, we need to celebrate." *Well, boys, a babysitter and alcohol are how I took that.*

Lisa began pouring the first drink when Allen came in. "Well, we are paid in full in a few weeks, the invoice has been provided." Nick nodded his head in approval and Lisa flung her hands up like she had just won the lottery.

Nick, Lisa and Allen all sat around drinking, with Lisa getting her buzz going first.

"Light weight?" Allen asked, but he didn't really need an answer. "Hey guys, I ordered dinner, and I need to walk to get it. I'll be back in an hour. Be good and don't pass out." That last statement was directed at Lisa, but he could tell she had been in this situation before, drinking to get drunk and then keeping her buzz going.

Lisa poured Allen a rather strong drink for the walk, and he left. In the meantime, her and Nick started sipping on their own. Nick had broken out his Woodford Reserve that he had half gone already.

"Oh, too good for my house liquors?" Lisa chuckled.

"I'm not in high school, little girl," Nick responded.

"No, but you did spank me like a principal," Lisa responded. This made Nick laugh. His mood had lightened since the case was solved and Lisa could tell.

"Yes, yes I did, and if you keep running your pretty mouth, that ass is going to be as red as the hood you wore on Halloween."

The tension built for the next fifteen minutes as they sat there talking about the case. But Lisa wasn't listening, and neither was Nick.

Suddenly the alcohol started talking through Lisa's lips, "Are you going to ever fuck me again? I wore a thong, thinking Allen might go to bed early."

"He might, he tends to do that, but why don't you come over here, and I'll let you make the first move this time. I like to relax with my bourbon."

Lisa smiled, caught off guard by his nicety of the situation.

"Get the fuck over here, slut," Nick said after her few seconds of hesitation. Yup, there was the dominant asshole that flooded her pussy when he spoke like that. "And that is why I take what I want, because when I offer it, you seem to think you get some sense of control."

Nick had pulled his cock out while she started coming over. Already half an erection showed before she made her way over. She began to lift her dress as Nick grabbed her head and pointed her mouth toward his cock. "No, no, you take care of me first, then I'll fuck you."

Lisa grabbed his cock with her fist and immediately took it into her mouth. She didn't know how big it really was until she realized that she couldn't take but maybe half in her mouth before gagging a little. She had seen it and felt it before, but she was in such a daze and so wet that she could have taken anything that night. This is when the dominant side of Nick took over, lightly pushing her head farther down. This made Lisa's eyes water and she loved every minute of it.

After a few minutes of Nick basically fucking her mouth, Lisa felt the grasp of Nick's hand as he lifted her up. He pulled up her dress to find out she was wearing the smallest thong she could. Nick's hands yanked them from her body with little effort. "Buy yourself a new pair on me," he said as he lifted Lisa into place, hovering over him while she guided it into her aching pussy. "Good girl," Nick added.

It startled Lisa for a moment as she started thrusting her hips because it made her think of how Allen says it to her. As if almost on cue, Allen opened the door, arriving back sooner than he had said. Lisa, startled and embarrassed, attempted to get off Nick, frantically trying to straighten herself up. She liked Allen, a lot and wanted him to think of her as a lady. But Nick wouldn't let her move, holding her still. Lisa was in such a daze that she eventually stopped resisting. Lisa was overcome with so many emotions that she didn't know what to do.

Suddenly, she could feel Nick's hand let go of her hair, replaced by Allen's. It immediately went from holding in place like a fuck doll to feeling Allen's hands run through her hair like a brush, straightening it out.

"There you go, sweet girl, I'm here for you." Allen's voice sent a calming through Lisa that her body went limp on Nick.

"We're best friends, Lisa, and the one thing that has kept us best friends since we were five years old" Nick said, his cock still rock hard inside her, "is we don't hide things from each other."

"That, and we share," Allen added, undoing his belt and pants.

In that instant Lisa knew. "Oh, fuck," she gasped, realizing that her efforts to hide her insane attraction to Nick from Allen and hiding her crush and desire to be held by Allen from Nick had been useless. *They both knew about each other all along.*

"Relax, pretty girl," Allen said, gently pushing his semi-hard cock into her mouth. "We'll take care of you."

"Very good care," Nick added, thrusted everything he had into her as she sat on him.

Lisa didn't know if that meant sexually or otherwise, but right now she imagined it was both. She was about to fuck both her dream alpha male and dream boyfriend at the same time. For the first time in her life, she was in love and in lust and didn't want the moment to end.

As her mouth began working on Allen's cock, she started to try to go deeper and deeper, her face starting to tear up again. Allen calmed her, stroking her hair while Nick thrusted from underneath. Her pussy was taking a pounding, and Nick's thrusting was pushing her mouth farther and farther toward Allen's cock. As Nick exploded in her pussy, she could feel it filling whatever void was left inside her, and what didn't fit started to run out onto Nick's cock. This made her cum with such loud moans that no doubt someone walking on the sidewalk outside could hear it.

The site of Nick fucking her and her intense orgasm caused Allen's excitement to build. Although completely exhausted, it was now Allen's slightly tightening grip on her hair that caused him to begin mouth fucking her. *Fuck whatever you want as hard as you want.* That was the language her body was speaking right now.

"Good girl, you take his cum down your throat," Nick said, encouraging her to take it as hard as Allen could give it and offer no resistance.

Suddenly Allen showed his own dominant side and forced her mouth all the way down. Lisa's makeup had become running down her eyes at this moment as she began to drool and gag on Allen's cock. "Good fucking girl Lisa," he said as she could tell by his actions he was about to cum.

Suddenly, her mouth was filled with Allen's cum as he moaned and flung his head back.

"There you go, little girl," Nick said, watching some ooze from her mouth.

Gasping for air, Lisa removed her mouth and looked at them both, wanting approval from both. In the past twenty minutes, Lisa had realized that there was a little bit of the dominant in Allen and a little bit of a daddy in Nick. They complemented each other perfectly, and she was in a place and a daze she had never been in.

Once Lisa had cleaned up all the cum with her mouth, all three of them positioned themselves such that Lisa could lay half on Nick and Allen could half spoon Lisa. After a few moments, once they all were able to relax and get back into reality, they cleaned up. It was a day to celebrate and a night they would never forget.

Epilogue

After that night Allen had told both Nick and Lisa that we were going to shut down the agency for a few weeks to take some much-needed time off. The case rattled them all and they all needed to take their own form of vacation. The money had cleared earlier than usual and Nick and Allen both decided Lisa get a cut as a bonus. She had helped solve the case and they wanted her to stick around.

Nick always did the same thing on his time away. The Navy had given him the opportunity to visit new places so once he found the one thing he liked doing most, he stuck with it. He loved going deep sea fishing down in Costa Rica and he always stayed at the same place. It had been updated some over the years but always provided that same level of familiarity he enjoyed. He had come so often that the locals recognized him. There was nothing more gratifying than hooking into a fish double or more his size and bringing it on the boat as if saying 'I beat you.'

Allen was more adventurous and liked to visit new places. During his time on the police force he was so into work that vacations consisted of sitting at a few tables in town or maybe visiting the beaches in

California. But with decent size bonuses and no one to tie him down, he decided the travel the world more often. From the Northern Lights in Alaska to the palace tours and beaches in Thailand to taking two weeks mingling with singles on Mediterranean cruises, Allen was living his best life and with money to spare.

Lisa used her bonus to take her boys to see some places they wouldn't have been able to on a waitress' salary. They went to Reno to stay with the great grandmother of the kids that they have absolutely fell in love with. Turns out she has a little money from a life insurance policy she cashed in on and with no bills, graciously accepted Lisa's offer to come on some of the trips. From the Grand Canyon to some of the sights Los Angeles had to offer, Lisa was able to provide for her boys in a way she didn't know was possible 6 months ago. In addition, Christmas was going to be much better than previous years past.

Once the two-week break was over and the office opened on that much cooler than before morning in mid-November, Sergeant Rick was waiting, this time in civilian clothes. "Come to celebrate with us?" Nick said, clearing the cobwebs from a little too much bourbon the night before. "Allen won't be here for another hour or so, flight got in late."

"A delivery truck was found across town," Sergeant Rick's gaze remained looking at the floor.

Nick didn't need him to say it, he could tell that they found bodies.

"This one involves families with children."

Printed in Great Britain
by Amazon